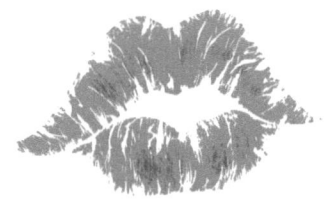

EVERNIGHT PUBLISHING ®

www.evernightpublishing.com

SAM CRESCENT

Copyright© 2021

Sam Crescent

Editor: Karyn White

Cover Art: Sour Cherry Designs

Jacket Design: Jay Aheer

ISBN: 978-0-3695-0309-1

ALL RIGHTS RESERVED

BROKEN HEARTS

DEDICATION

As always, I want to thank Evernight Publishing for giving Chaos Bleeds a home, and also my wonderful editor. They really are amazing.

BROKEN HEARTS

BROKEN HEARTS

Chaos Bleeds, 7

Sam Crescent

Copyright © 2015

Prologue

Dick in rehab

Dick's entire body was hurting. He didn't like pain, and the only way to deal with that was to snort up, or inject some hard shit into his veins. Any other time he'd have already been high as a fucking kite, but he wasn't allowed. No, not anymore. This was the new rule of the club, Chaos Bleeds. Devil needed him, them all, to be clean. To stay in the club, he had to be clean, no more drugs for him. They were up against a worse enemy, and none of them could stop what was about to happen. Devil needed them all to be safe, and being an addict didn't help the club, it only failed the club. Dick didn't want his brothers to see him like this. The shakes were the worst, the constant itching, and his body felt like it wasn't his own. He'd never felt like this before, and he didn't know what was worse, the sickness, or the need that was like fire in his veins.

Butler was already on the road to recovery while Dick was still trying to figure his shit out. He hated it, and everything else that was going on. There were times he wondered if he should just quit the club, but he couldn't do it. Chaos Bleeds meant everything to him, and turning his back on them wasn't in him to do. The club was all he had.

Keeping the blanket wrapped around him, Dick was pulled out of his pity party, and drawn to the commotion coming from the corner.

"You fucking whore. I don't want to be here. I don't need to be here. I'm fine, and you know it. You're just jealous that I get all the cock while you get nothing, you fat bitch."

Dick snorted as he watched Becky storm out of the room. The girl was a candidate for syringes and sticking shit in her veins, just like him. She was slender, skin and bone really from lack of food, and all the drugs she would take. He eyed the sister who kept making an appearance. It didn't matter how many times Becky mouthed off, spit and cursed, her sister always came back to the rehab center for more. No one else came in to see Becky, but Martha, she came to see her regularly, without fail. The rock who stood beside her destructive sister. It was sad to see.

Martha sat down on the chair, looking forlorn.

"You shouldn't take the shit she's saying to heart," he said, not understanding why he was telling her anything. He didn't make anyone feel better. He was far happier causing problems than helping.

"She does mean it."

"No. It's the withdrawal. It's a fucking bitch."

"You're not looking much good yourself," she said.

He shrugged. "I'm doing the best I can with the shit that I got."

She giggled. "You're insane, and crazy."

"Nah, name's Dick," he said.

Martha moved a little closer, and shook his hand. "Your name is Dick? That doesn't sound right to me. It's not really a name."

"It's my name."

She shook her head. "Becky told me you were part of some MC gang. It's your road name. She also told me you've got a reputation for being a huge dick. Your name matches your attitude."

"Becky talks too much."

"Not really. She needs to talk more, and get everything out in the open. She doesn't, and that just sucks." Martha slumped down into the seat opposite him, without an invitation to do so. "What's your real name?"

"I'm not telling you."

"Why?"

"You'd laugh, and I don't like being laughed at."

"You can't be serious?" she asked. Dick didn't respond, and only glared at her. "I'm now more intrigued than ever. What is your name?"

Her smile was the most beautiful thing he'd ever seen. Her eyes twinkled, and she wasn't looking at him like a piece of shit. Dick couldn't recall the last time a woman looked at him as if he was a person. The whores back at the club served him as they were owned by the club, not because they wanted him. He didn't want their skanky pussy most of the time, but it scratched an itch and he didn't have to go hunting for it.

"You do know I'm in here because I've got the same problem as your sister?" he asked.

"What? You can't say no to a high? Yeah, I get that. I'm not going to stop coming and seeing my sister.

You deal with your problems in any way you can. I get that. I even understand it." She shrugged. "I deal with mine through food. I eat a lot."

Tilting his head to the side, Dick shook his head, and didn't have a clue as to why he was about to tell her his name. He didn't tell anyone his name. "Fine, my name is Teddy. T.E.D.D.Y."

"Why would I laugh at that?"

Gritting his teeth, he stared at her. "My last name is Bear. B.E.A.R."

He saw the moment she understood why she'd laugh. Dick even expected it. After all, his name had been the source of many people's entertainment.

"Teddy Bear, wow, your, erm, your folks really knew what they were doing, didn't they?"

"Dick's much easier to deal with, and I like the name. I use my dick every chance I get."

Martha sat back smiling at him. "Well, it's nice to see you, Teddy Bear, Dick."

They shook hands, and Dick couldn't believe he'd told her the truth about his name. He didn't tell anyone. There were brothers he rode with who didn't even know the truth of his name. It was all fucking horseshit, and wrong.

He hated it, hated his name.

When he was growing up he'd gotten into so many fights and arguments. He'd lost count of the number of times he'd ambled home after a day of fighting at school.

After that moment whenever Martha came to see Becky, she'd always spend an hour or two chatting with him. She really believed that Becky was on the road to recovery, and was planning on getting her a job and an apartment when she was out. He didn't have the heart to tell her that one of the doctors was giving Becky shit on the side, and in return she was giving him everything he wanted, blowjobs, sex, anal. Dick had gone to the toilet the other day and discovered Becky bent over the counter taking it up the ass all in the name of getting a little smack. Dick liked his ass the way it was, and he also loved his club. He didn't ask for anything while he was on the inside. Martha was blind to what was happening. When she was with him, he didn't want to upset her. She was just sweet, nice, and he didn't want to change that. Martha was refreshing to him.

He even called Devil up, and asked him to deal with the bastard who was taking what he wanted from Becky.

Martha helped Dick to get clean. Talking with her, laughing with her, it all helped for him to know what he wanted out of life. Waiting for her to visit was what got him to remain clean, to stay clean every single hour of every single day, even when he wanted to give in, and fuck the world. Remembering Martha's smiling face made him stronger, and he fought the need, and stayed clean.

Finally, when he left the rehabilitation center, Martha was there to congratulate him, hug him goodbye, and for the first time in his life, he didn't want to be a Dick to her. She'd been through enough, and didn't need anything else.

"If you ever need me," he said, "come and find me. I'll help you out."

"I'm a good girl through and through. If you ever need to talk, come and find me. I like you, Teddy, even if you don't think you deserve to be liked." She quickly grabbed a piece of paper out of her bag, and wrote down the details he'd need. "Anytime. Come and visit."

"I will. Take care, honey."

"You, too."

He left her, and didn't look back, not once. Why didn't he need to? He was a dick, and Martha deserved better.

Chapter One

Dick slammed into Lydia, watching as his condom-slick cock opened up her tight little pussy. She was screaming like a fucking banshee, which was really starting to grate on his last nerve. She didn't even sound all that great. The noise was giving him a headache, and with his past addictions, he couldn't take fucking painkillers. He'd been wrong about Lydia. Totally fucking wrong. He'd actually thought Lydia was the one woman for him. She took his shit, and gave back just as much, yet it wasn't working. He couldn't stand her. She was irritating, needy, demanding, and she just pissed him off all the time.

"Please, Dick, harder. Fuck me like you mean it."

It had been over a year since she was taken by the fucker known as Master. In that time, Death, Snake, and the whole of the club had been on the search for the mysterious man who took women, used and abused them, before tossing them away. The man they were searching for was like a damn ghost. One moment he was there, the next moment he was gone, puffed into smoke.

"I need it. I need you."

He was getting fucking tired of hearing her voice. At first he'd wanted to help her, to get her friends with Jessica once again. Instead, her voice was grating on his nerves. He hated the way she sounded, and her entire presence in his life was pissing him off. He hated her, hated everything she stood for, and he hated fucking her.

Gripping her hips, he pumped into her several times until he found his own release. Lydia squealed her own orgasm as she'd been fingering her pussy the entire time. When he was finished, he collapsed over her and simply took a breath. He rarely helped her to orgasm, and only ever took what he wanted. After sex, he liked quiet, and to simply enjoy the release of his cum, even if it wasn't in a cunt he wanted.

Then she started talking.

"That was amazing," she said. "Really, Dick, you certainly know how to use what's been given to you. I bet your daddy was packing, wasn't he?"

She went ahead and spoiled everything with her mouth. He had really made a big mistake. Pulling out of her pussy, he tore the condom from his dick, and stormed into his bathroom. He kept his door open, and out of the corner of his eye he could keep an eye on her. There was no way he'd let Lydia out of his sight. He didn't trust her for a second.

You trusted Martha.

He stared at his reflection and couldn't stop thinking about the woman who'd invaded his thoughts often since leaving rehab.

"Come on, Dick, I want to go again."

"Fuck off."

He ran a hand down his face, and tried his hardest to look at the man in the mirror staring right back at him. Where the fuck had Martha come from? He'd not seen or heard of her in the last couple of years since he'd gotten out of rehab. The last thing he wanted to do was deal with that kind of shit in his life. No matter how hard he tried, he kept coming back to the same thoughts about her. He had liked Martha. She'd been sweet, funny, and just refreshing, like taking a breath of fresh air.

Lydia moved up behind him, running her hands all over his back, around his waist. "You don't mean that."

"Get the fuck out of my bedroom."

"Come on, we're practically dating."

"We're not fucking dating." He grabbed her arms and shoved her away. "We're not doing anything. We're just screwing around. Don't think for a fucking instant that this makes you my old lady. It doesn't. It doesn't make you anything to me. You hear me?"

Lydia let out a sigh as if he was a child. "Whatever you say, Dick."

She turned on her heel and walked out. Dick didn't like the way she was behaving as if she owned the place. He'd never made a claim on her, and he had been wrong. Lydia was not the one for him. He was done with her. Dick couldn't fucking stand her, and there was no way he was ever having her as an old lady. He'd tried to do a good thing, and she was the only woman besides Martha who handled his dick attitude. The difference between Lydia and Martha was that Lydia was just a big of a dick as he was, only she had a pussy instead of a dick. Damn, he missed Martha.

He took a quick shower, and dressed in another pair of jeans, not bothering with a shirt. There were old scars around his arms from being a past user, and he'd thought about covering them up with ink. Instead, he kept them on display, so everyone knew who he was. Dick wasn't ashamed of his past as an addict. It was what had saved him during those years, and now, it was the club that saved him.

Tugging on some boots, he made his way downstairs to find Snake, Jessica, Brianna, and Death sitting at the bar, drinking.

He walked into the kitchen where Lexie was making some hot chocolate for the little ones.

"Damn, why don't you put your arms away?" Lexie said.

"Kids should know what will happen to them if they start shooting shit up." Dick gave Simon a wink, and the young boy smiled. They didn't keep anything from the club. "You should consider me a walking advertisement of what not to do with their life."

"Seriously, enough. They're my kids, and I'll tell you what they can and cannot handle." Lexie gave him a look that only mothers seemed to possess. It was that look that said, "If you fuck with me, I will fuck with you back. The difference? I'm going to make your life a living hell a lot longer than you'll ever make mine."

"Okay, they're your kids. I'm going to get myself a sandwich." When he found one made up, he took it, leaving the kitchen. He gave Simon a high-five on the way out.

"That was my sandwich for work today," Jessica said.

"Sorry. You'll have to deal with canteen food. You're a nurse. I'm hungry, I come first."

"Asshole."

"You love me for it."

"I'd love you even more if you'd stop fucking that bitch." Jessica held onto Snake's arms as she shot a glare across the room to Lydia.

"She's got a great pussy, and she's willing to open her legs for me. Consider her easy pickings."

"I hope you find a woman that makes you work for it. You're a pig," Jessica said.

"You're just encouraging him now," Snake said, kissing his woman's neck. "Leave him to make his own bad decisions."

"Yeah, and I bet he'll get a hard-on." Jessica scrunched up her nose before turning to leave. "I've got to go."

He watched the women leave, and he stood with Death, Snake, and Butler who'd come close to the bar.

"Do we have any news on Master?" Death asked, changing the subject quickly.

No one wanted to bring up the bastard's name

because of what he had done to Brianna and to Jessica. Dick wouldn't even bring the bastard up. It was too much to see the women in pain. He'd been part of the retrieval for Jessica and Lydia. That shit had been messed up. He was a dick to the core, but he didn't pick on women. Women were meant to be kept out of mess. He'd never raise his fist to a woman or do anything to hurt them, which was one of the reasons Lydia pissed him off. There was nothing he could do about it. Living with her would be a nightmare, and he was thankful that he'd not made her his old lady.

"No. Whizz isn't much help either. He can't go on a ghost, and so far, Master is a ghost. Whizz said that he needed more than a name, and the vague description that we've got. His computer skills don't allow him to pull something out of thin air. We're even calling him fucking Master, so I don't know how we're going to help," Snake said. "I want to kill him. I want to hurt him in ways he's hurt my woman. Whatever Master has done, I want him fucking dead."

Jessica had ended up with a scar on the inside of her thigh because of the brand Master had put on her leg. He'd used a branding iron or something like that. Brianna, Jessica, and Lydia all had them. All three women had ink over their marks so they didn't have to see the brand any longer. Unlike his own scars, he admired the three women for inking over their scars. It was an awful thing to have to remember, and he hoped it helped the women to heal.

"We've got to wait for him to resurface," Dick said. "I've spoken to all of the women at the strip club, and I've been in contact with the women who we rescued from Gonzalez. The ones who bore the same mark of the branding iron couldn't give anything away. They knew nothing about him. It was like he didn't exist. This is how he's stayed quiet all these years. No one really knows him."

"We've got to find him. He's dangerous," Snake said.

"I know, and he's far more dangerous than us," Dick said.

"Why's that?" Death asked.

"We can be found easily. He knows where we are, and we know fuck all about him. It makes him pretty fucking dangerous, and us seem like pussies." Dick took another bite out of his sandwich. He'd make another one for Jessica, and Snake knew it.

The sound of a squealing baby had all the men turning toward the stairs. Ripper was walking down with his son, Paul. Nine months ago Judi and Paul had almost died because of pre-eclampsia. Fortunately, Judi had pulled through, and so had Paul, their son.

"You're not waking Mommy up. You've kept her awake the past three nights, and you're going to learn to take your milk from Daddy."

"What's wrong?" Snake asked.

"Judi needs sleep, but this little guy is determined to wake her up. I didn't know it, but he's been keeping her up half of the night to feed him, so then through the day, she's exhausted, and she's going to end up ill. I won't let that happen. Judi hates hospitals, and that's where she'll end up if this little guy won't let her have sleep." Ripper held his son with one arm, and Paul was sucking on the flesh on the inside of his arm.

Dick finished off the sandwich then made his way into the kitchen at the same time as Ripper.

"I don't suppose you'll hold him while I prepare his food?" Ripper asked.

"You want me to hold your son?"

"It's not hard. You're my brother, and you'll die

for me."

"I know, but I've never held a kid."

"He's not," Lexie said, bustling her kids out of the kitchen. "He refused to help me with mine."

Before he could say anything, Lexie had already taken the kids out of the way. He was the only one left to hold Paul. "Fuck," he said. "Fine, give me your kid. Tell me how to hold him."

"It's quite simple. You need to support his whole body, and his head. The way I had him keeps him safely tucked up."

"Shit, man." Dick didn't like the thought of the kid resting against his old scars, and so he held onto his head, supporting his whole body with his arms. He held the kid away from him, and stared into the innocence of his blue eyes. The little guy was going to be a handsome fucker, like his mom and dad. Dick was uncomfortable, and he didn't want any of his evil to rub off on the little guy.

"He's not infected. You can hold him close. He won't start to wriggle. Only if he thinks you're not holding him right does he wriggle."

Dick changed the way he was holding him, and smiled down a Paul.

"See, it's not so hard," Ripper said.

Paul had stopped crying, and the silence hung in the air.

"What's wrong with him?" Dick asked.

"Nothing. You're holding him close, and you're new." Ripper started pulling out a bottle from the fridge and testing it. "You're a natural with him."

"No, I'm not."

"You are. I've never seen him be so quiet before. Will you and Lydia be having kids?" Ripper asked.

"No. I'm not making that whore my old lady."

"Then you better make her realize that. She's going around telling everyone she's your old lady."

"Fuck, man, between her and this shit with Master, I need a damn break."

"Are you tripping?" Ripper asked.

"No. I don't need to go back on my word. What I need is to get away."

Go to Martha. Go see her.

Dick didn't like the way she was invading his thoughts, and taking over his life. For a long time he'd not thought about her. It had been over three years since he got out of rehab, and hadn't needed to go back. The club had kept him sane, and he'd not even been tempted to go back on his word, and take drugs again.

"Hey, fuckers," Butler said, walking into the kitchen. "Dime, Spider, Sinner, and Slash are back. We went looking around the old mansion where we found Lydia and Jessica. No luck. Everything that was there is gone."

Dime, Spider, Sinner, and Slash were usually great at picking up scents and finding people that didn't want to be found. They came as a team, and used to be in the Seals. They'd had a bad time of it in the service, and when they got out years ago, they joined Chaos Bleeds, and never looked back. Guts and Sexy, two other guys, had ended up in rehab as well, not with him but at a different facility.

Since they'd settled down in Piston County, they'd all changed. It was insane, crazy, and yet it wasn't. The Skulls had changed, and they'd been in Fort Wills for years. It would only make sense that all clubs change eventually even though they don't want to.

Dick couldn't believe he'd gone from being an addict to clean, and now he was talking about a break. The only problem was it wasn't a break away from the club. He needed to go and see Martha, to see how she was handling Becky. The moment he left the rehab center, he'd cut off all contact with his life, with Martha. He'd thought about her from time to time, but he'd not felt the need to make sure she was okay. That had changed in the last couple of hours. He wanted to go see her, and it was like a need burning up inside him.

"You need a break, talk to Devil. He'll understand. You've done everything he's ever asked you, and I know I appreciate that, and so will he." Ripper handed him the bottle. "Feed him and I'll make Jessica a replacement sandwich."

"You've conned me."

"No. I'm trying to prove to you that not all women are animals, or bitches, or after your dick."

He took the bottle from Ripper, and started to feed Paul. The kid wouldn't look away from him. He was so cute, and adorable, and he just knew if he didn't get out soon, he'd be made a babysitter. The kid was cute, but then, to him, all kids were cute.

"Lydia's not all bitch." He didn't know why he was defending her. Dick himself could be a bastard, so wasn't it the same thing?

"Yes, she is. She almost got herself and Jessica killed. It's only because of Jessica that Snake went after her. Any real friend would have made sure they don't know shit. Lydia's not good enough for you, Dick."

Gritting his teeth, he forced himself to look at Ripper. "What makes you think I'm good enough for anyone? I'm an ex-addict, Ripper. I've worked for my next score. I've killed people, and I don't give a fuck about anything."

"And yet even high, you've had my back. Okay, so it wasn't as clear as it is now, but you've had my back when I needed you. You've protected the women when you've needed to. You're not some asshole who doesn't deserve to be happy. Fuck, Judi felt for a long time that she couldn't be loved because of what happened in her life. It took me a long time to prove to her that she deserved love."

Judi was one of the first women they met when they came to Piston County. She was underage, and being forced to prostitute herself, abused at every corner. The Chaos Bleeds crew had taken her in, loved her, and she was one of theirs. Ripper and Judi had ended up falling in love with Ripper almost getting killed when the truth came out. It had been some seriously messed up shit, but no one would change it. Ripper had proven to everyone that he loved Judi.

"Judi shouldn't have ever felt like that," Dick said.

"She did, and it took me time to get her to realize she could be loved."

"It's still fucking wrong."

"I know. It sucks." He shrugged. "I've gotten through to her, and now we're good."

Spider chose that moment to come into the kitchen sitting with Butler.

"What's going on?"

"I'm thinking of stopping by Naked Fantasies," Spider said. He glanced up at the clock. "It's still open."

Dick frowned as he looked at Spider. They had all agreed to keep Naked Fantasies as the name for the strip club that the Chaos Bleeds club owned. Vincent still ran the club, only everything was aboveboard now, after the Gonzalez incident. Dick's life was getting complicated with everything going on with the club, and Lydia.

"Why?" Butler asked. "It's closed in an hour. What the fuck are you going to do?"

"Fuck off." Spider stormed back out of the kitchen, leaving them all confused.

Staring down at Paul, Dick finished feeding him while Ripper prepared Jessica's sandwich for work. They all appreciated the work she did. If it wasn't for her, Judi may not be sleeping upstairs, and he may not be holding Paul in his arms.

"He's finished," Dick said, holding the empty bottle up.

"Okay, you need to burp him now."

After ten minutes of being told how to burp a baby, Dick was going to have a breakdown. He needed to get out of the club. Once Paul had given them multiple burps, he handed him back to Ripper, and made his way up to his room. Lydia was nowhere to be seen, which he was thankful for. He didn't want to deal with that bitch. Once inside his room, he locked the door. No one was going to disturb him now.

You made a mistake, and you shouldn't have let her draw you in.

****

Spider leaned against the outside of Naked Fantasies waiting for *her* to come out. She wasn't like the other women who danced at the club. Her stage name was Beauty, but her real name was Paris. From the moment she stood on the stage and started dancing he'd been hypnotized by her. She wasn't like the other women who were trying to gain the guys' attention. Paris didn't look at any of them. She didn't hang out, and she was always the first woman to leave the club. Some of the brothers liked to stay after the doors closed, getting some of the freebies that the girls offered.

None of the boys could come up with a new name for the club, and so they'd stuck with the old name.

The door opened, and he was in the shadows so

she didn't see him immediately. She wore a hoodie over her head, and a pair of torn jeans. The sensual woman from the stage was long gone. The door closed, and Paris was about to step past him when Spider stepped out of the shadows.

"Hello," he said.

She screamed and held her hands up, prepared to fight him. "What the fuck?" she asked, pushing her hoodie back.

"Why are you coming back here alone?" he asked.

"I always come back here alone, Spider." She crossed her arms over her chest. "What's the problem?"

"Nothing. I just thought you'd like a ride home."

"No. I'm good. The last time I checked, I remembered where I lived." She made to start walking, but Spider caught her arms, stopping her.

"I'm offering you a ride."

"I don't want one."

"Why are you being such a bitch?" he asked.

"I'm not. Why are you determined to talk to me? I don't know you. When I signed my contract with Naked Fantasies it didn't say anything about giving freebies to the owners."

"I'm not asking for freebies."

"What are you asking for then?"

"The chance to give you a ride." He folded his own arms, waiting for her to refuse him. Paris wouldn't ever give him the time of day, nor would she give any of the guys her time. She kept them all at a distance, and it was just another aspect of her that enthralled him.

"You're not going to back down, are you?" she asked.

"No. I'm not."

She released a sigh. "Look, I know some of the

women want your attention, and I get it. I'm not one of those women. I don't need your attention, and I don't want it either."

"Since when is offering a ride something more?"

"I don't know. I don't want you getting the wrong idea."

"I'm not going to get the wrong idea. You don't want anything to do with me, fine. I'm offering you a ride home. It's pretty dangerous for a beautiful woman, and I was offering my protection. Where's the harm in that?"

She stared at him for several minutes, and finally caved. "Fine. We're only having a ride though, right?"

"Yes."

Spider wanted to punch the air at what he'd achieved. Paris was different from anyone he'd ever met. He usually liked his pussy to be easy so he didn't have to work at it. The women who stripped in the club didn't appeal. Paris was the only woman he liked to watch. She pulled the club into the dance and the movement of her body. Most of the time she didn't even need to strip off all of her clothes, only making it down to her underwear before the music stopped. Other times, she teased some men with showing her nakedness while other men were left wanting more. Paris had been spoken to about it, but they couldn't argue with her when she said it brought customers back. It fucking did. They were all hoping to see who would finally get Beauty. She was dramatic, beautiful, and her curves were addictive. He wanted to get his hands on her curves.

Some of the women were catty about her. He'd heard them referring to her as "the fat one". They had learned never to say that kind of shit to him. He protected her the best way he could.

Again, he didn't have a fucking clue as to why he

did it. She was ungrateful for his services.

Chapter Two

The following day Dick watched as Devil was working on his bike. Simon was standing with him, and the two were chatting. The young boy was in school, and Dick knew that Lexie and Devil had been called to the school about Simon's behavior. Simon was a lot like his father. He didn't like to be told what to do, spoke his mind, and tried to fool all of the teachers. It was great around the club, but in school, it was proving to be difficult.

"What's going on?" Butler asked.

"I'm wondering when the best time to go and talk to Devil is." Dick took a sip of his coffee, watching father and son work. "He's been sent home again. Lexie pulled up an hour ago, dropping Simon off for Devil to talk to him. The school isn't happy with his behavior."

"Boy's going to need to learn when to do shit he doesn't like," Butler said.

"I know."

"I'm heading out."

He placed the empty cup down on the nearest table. One of the club whores could clean it up. Dick made his way out of the clubhouse toward Devil and Simon.

"But I don't want to do as they tell me. They're thick and stupid. They're not club, Dad. I only listen to the club," Simon said.

"Look, son, you've got to do what you're told at school. I've told you this. Don't take fucking shit from anyone else, and just take it easy. I can't handle your mother bitching at me about this. You need to go to school. You need to learn."

Simon went to open his mouth, but Devil held his hand up.

27

"I love you, son. That's never going to change. I'll love you if you're thick and stupid, or if you're clever. You want a chance at running this club when you're older?"

Simon nodded.

"Then get your fucking head down at school. Get the grades, 'cause I'm warning you, I won't leave my club in the hands of a fool."

"But, Dad!"

"Don't 'but Dad' me, boy. I'm tired of you being lazy. If Tabitha was going to school here, you'd be there in a heartbeat. Don't fucking try the shit with me, do you hear?"

"Yes."

"Besides, Tabitha will not want your ass if you don't know how to spell her name."

"I know how to spell her name!"

"Then make sure you can spell more than her name." Devil glared at his son. The two were just butting heads.

"Leave him, Devil," Dick said, taking a seat beside Simon. "Tabitha will pass Simon over. I bet The Skulls will have more than enough prospects for her to look at. The ones that can spell every word in the dictionary. I heard girls like that. You know, clever guys. It's the ones who can't spell who come out last."

"No, she won't date any of them. She's mine. Tabitha's my old lady." Simon shouted the words, and jumped down from the wall.

"Where are you going?" Devil asked.

"To do my homework, and write an apology letter to the principal, my teacher, and to Mom."

Devil waited for Simon to disappear inside the clubhouse before laughing. "Damn, that boy is pussy whipped, and he's fucking six years old. Fucking nightmare."

"At least you've got a girl to hang over him. Just bribe him with Tabitha. He'll come running."

"I shouldn't have to be using that young girl. She started school this September. My son is into his second year, and she's in her first. This is going to be a problem."

"Why?"

"Tabitha's a Skull. Simon's a Chaos. The two don't mesh."

"I thought you and Tiny were getting over your problems," Dick said.

"We are, but it's not the same. He insulted my club. Nothing is ever right after that. I'm only doing what I do to help Lexie. She wants to stay friends with Eva, and that's fine with me. It's why we went to that stupid prom."

"They'll lose interest," Dick said.

"I don't know." Devil looked toward the house. "Simon's stubborn. I'll have to watch him when he grows up." They fell silent as Devil finished fixing his bike. "What can I help you with?"

"What makes you think I want anything?"

"It's lunchtime, and you're out here instead of in there. You never look for me. Ever since I demanded you go to rehab, you've not come and looked for me."

Dick hadn't thought of that. When the rule first came out of get clean, or get out of the club, he'd been nervous as hell. At first he'd not wanted to go to rehab. He liked getting high instead of dealing with the shit in the world. Then he thought about what he actually had in life. He didn't have fucking anything in life, not really. All he cared about was Chaos Bleeds. It was his life, his world, and he wasn't going to let that change. So he'd gone and got cleaned, pissed about having to change who he was. Chaos Bleeds didn't change for anyone, but faced with an enemy like Gonzalez, who could ruin them, he'd done his part. Dick hadn't really thought about his reaction to Devil. He'd not gone out of his way to be friends with him, but then, Devil was a busy man. He spent half of his time knocking Lexie up.

"I'm sorry."

"Don't be sorry. Just tell me what you want to say, and I'll deal with it." Devil stood up wiping his hands on a cloth. "I'm not the kind of man to start crying over shit. I did what I had to do, and I did it to protect the club and my men. I'll do it again, and I'll keep doing it until the day I die. When I pass over my club, I'll never stop looking out for it."

"I've not had a problem staying clean."

"I know that. If you did, you'd go straight back to rehab."

"Thanks. The thing is, I need a break away from everything."

"A break?" Devil asked.

"Yeah. It has been a couple of years since I was in rehab, and I met someone there. I want to go and see if she's okay."

"You want to go and see a woman?"

"Yeah."

"A woman in rehab?"

"No, her sister. I got talking to her, and she made life easier. She helped me."

Devil stared at him, which Dick hated.

"What?" he asked.

"Nothing. I'm just thinking about you, and a woman. She didn't try to kill you?"

"No, she didn't. I can be nice when I need to be."

"Okay," Devil said, holding his hands up. "I'm not your keeper, and I'll believe you. Go and visit her. If you go through other MC territory, remove your cut. I'm not interested in starting wars. You know the drill. I'm not your momma or anything. Take care, and keep us updated."

Dick agreed. He must be getting old. There was a time when he would have been happy to start a fight with someone. "I'm going to head out at the end of the day."

"You're not going to phone ahead."

"No. I want to just get it over and done with." If Martha was married with a guy, he wanted to see it with his own two eyes.

"If you two were friends, then you shouldn't worry about just turning up."

"I'm not just worried about it," Dick said. "I've got to do this my way."

"Fine. Whatever you decide is up to you. Keep in touch."

He nodded, turning to leave.

"Teddy," Devil said, calling Dick by his actual name.

"What?"

"I'm proud of you. I wanted you to know that. I'm proud of you, and what you've done for this club."

Dick nodded. "Thank you."

He didn't like the emotion that was clogging up his throat. No one was ever proud of him, and he didn't like the way it was leaving him. He didn't give a shit what anyone thought of him. The last thing he wanted to do was think about being part of the Chaos Bleeds. Dick didn't do well with tears. They never helped in any situation.

Dick made his way up to his room, and started to pack. On his way out of the door, he was stopped by Lydia leaning against the doorframe. He didn't want her, and couldn't believe he ever had.

"I heard you're leaving," she said.

"I am."

"What do you want me to do while you're gone?"

"Do whatever the fuck you want."

"You really meant what you said? I'm not your old lady."

Dick let out a sigh, and stared at her. She was a pretty woman, but on the inside she was so fucking selfish. He was surprised that Jessica had stayed friends with her for so long. "I wanted to help you out. You looked so sad when Jessica broke off your friendship."

"You were helping me out of pity?"

"What did you want me to say or even do, Lydia?"

"Be an asshole."

"Fine, I wanted to fuck your pussy, but it wasn't as good as I thought it was going to fucking be. I'm moving on. You move on. It was never about love. I can't stand you."

"Fine." Lydia stormed off, and Dick simply left his room. He locked the door, and Jessica came out of the room opposite him.

"You listen to that?" he asked.

"Yes."

"Are you going to treat me like shit?"

"No. It makes sense that you were trying to help. You're not as big of a dick as you let everyone believe."

"You're a fucking idiot if you think I'm anything but a fucking idiot. How did you become a nurse?"

"Nah, I think you're okay." Jessica smiled at him, ignoring his jibe about her being a nurse. "Thank you for the sandwich."

"I didn't fucking make it," he said.

"No, but Ripper made it while you were feeding Paul. He wouldn't have made it, you would." Jessica kissed his cheek. "Thank you."

He didn't like it, but he didn't say anything. Dick would always replace what he took.

"I'm heading out."

"Ride safely. Regardless of what you think, Dick, you will be missed."

Dick made his way out of the clubhouse with several of the brothers talking with him, wishing him a good ride. Part of him didn't want to go, but he had to. There was only so much he could take. He needed a break, to get away from the crap that was happening in the club.

I need to see Martha.

Within the hour, he was on the road, and not looking back. He didn't want to talk to Martha before he made his way to her home. If she moved on then he wouldn't have to see her. The risk was too high of her answering if he phoned her. He wanted to be able to leave without hurting her.

He was messed up in the head, but it was his kind of logic, which made the most sense to him.

****

Martha wiped the sweat from her brow sitting back from the potatoes she was weeding through. She loved making her own kitchen style garden. The only reason she went to the store nowadays was to get milk, meat, and stuff she couldn't grow in her garden. If pizza grew from plants, she'd be set. She wasn't that bad though. She hadn't started milling her own flour. This was the place her parents had handed down to her and to Becky in their will. Her parents had learned how to work the stock markets so that they could live out in the middle of nowhere without any fear of the outside world coming in. They'd lived a reclusive life, which Martha didn't have a problem with.

Between her and Becky, Martha had taken to the reclusive lifestyle a hell of a lot easier than Becky. They were two completely different people. She wasn't cut off from the world in all elements. She had electricity, gas, and a television, along with a laptop, internet connection, and a way of contacting the outside world. Her neighbors weren't close, and it was hard for people to find her place out in the middle of nowhere, hidden by large trees and hedges.

Staring up at the sun in the sky, Martha took a breath then went back to digging through the dirt. She liked her potato plants to be free of weeds. They hadn't been hit by blight, which was a relief. Some of her plants hadn't worked, and she'd been lacking in the feeding and watering department. She was no expert, and everything she knew she'd learned from her parents and their books.

Once she was finished, she grabbed the large tub of weeds and took them to her compost heap. After she was done, she made her way back inside to get herself some iced tea.

"This is what you're doing all day?" Lynne asked, scaring Martha, causing her to scream.

Lynne Levy sat at her kitchen table, holding a glass of iced tea in her hand. Martha had gone to school with Lynne, and they had grown up together.

"What the fuck are you doing here?"

She and Lynne were best friends, even if they were worlds apart. Where Martha loved staying at home, leaving the world at bay, Lynne loved city life. She relished being involved in the world, competing to be the best damn lawyer in the country.

"You don't have to be rude, Martha. We have a date, remember? We're supposed to be heading into town tonight, partying it up. We arranged this three weeks ago."

Martha hit her head. "Shit, I forgot to put it on my calendar."

"I don't care. I've turned down a chance to take on a new divorce case tonight because I opted to be with my friend." Lynne took a sip of tea. "You still make the best tea I've ever tasted."

"Well, thank you for putting me into your busy schedule."

"Look, we're different, I get that. I respect your way of life, and I don't try to change you, Martha. Don't try and change me, and don't try to push me away. I'm not going to deal with it. We're friends, and it's time for you to live with that."

"I'm sorry. I'm an awful friend."

"You are."

"Okay, we're going out and partying tonight."

"Yes, so get your butt upstairs, and get out of that awful gardening crap. My eyes are going to be scarred for life over what I see you wearing. Go on, get changed. Make yourself actually look like a woman."

Laughing, Martha left her friend alone while she made her way up to her room. She removed her clothes, placing them into the laundry basket after she was done. Martha took time to clean beneath her nails. She really should wear gloves, but remembering them was a nightmare. Martha wasn't trying to impress anyone out in the middle of nowhere. This was her life, and she loved it the way it was.

After thirty minutes she looked normal, and was able to start getting ready to go out. Lynne wouldn't let her slip away no matter how much she wanted to. She'd been Martha's rock for so long, and she didn't want to lose her only friend.

Lynne was downstairs flicking through the television when Martha made her appearance. She'd gone for a pair of jeans, a tight red shirt, and left her brown hair down but curled it, to give it some form of a style. It was the best she was going to get.

"How do I look?"

While she'd been gone Lynne had changed into a skirt and very revealing top that showed off the globes of her breasts.

"You look beautiful. What's wrong with showing off some leg?"

"I'm not in the mood to show off my legs." She'd cut them while shaving. Martha didn't want to let her friend know that it had been two weeks since she last shaved. She had to remember to do it, as otherwise she was going to start having nightmares about the foliage she grew in certain places.

Lynne walked up to her. "It's not your fault, honey. You don't need to stop living your life because of Becky."

"I know. It's nothing. I know that. Don't mention it."

"Come on, let's go and kick back, have some fun, and maybe I can get a couple of smiles out of you before the night is over."

Martha chuckled, following Lynne out to her car. "What are we going to do for a lift?"

"You're not drinking. You never drink. You can drive my car back with both of us. We may be out to have some fun tonight, but I'm not leaving with some asshole. You must protect me. I demand it."

Shaking her head, Martha climbed into the passenger side of the car. She was so damn tired all the time.

"What's the matter?" Lynne asked.

"Nothing. I'm fine, really."

Lynne gave her a look that told her she wasn't

happy with the answer.

"I've missed you."

"There's nothing wrong with visiting me in the city. You won't get cooties or anything like that. You may find you like it. We're normal human beings."

"I don't want to. Look what happened to Becky."

"Becky was a first class bitch. I'm sorry, but you can't live your life through guilt. Becky took life her own way. You really should start living yours. You ever thought about what you're going to do later in life with a family? How are you going to meet that guy who'll give you children?"

"When I'm ready, I'll find him. I'm just not ready. Stop pushing."

Martha had hidden away the last two years. It had been hard from the moment Becky got out of rehab. Her thoughts drifted to Teddy, or Dick, which he preferred to be called. She'd not heard from him in so long.

You've not heard from him the moment he left rehab.

He was such a strong man and so different from the kind of men she was used to.

"What's got that smile on your face?"

"Nothing. I was just remembering a guy. He was nice, but he liked people to think he was a dick, and he acted like it."

"Sounds like a rather strange man. I thought your kink was the guy next door?"

"I don't have a kink, or a kind of guy I like. I've not got any of that," Martha said. She wondered if Dick was still on the straight and narrow, or if he'd kicked it all in, and started using.

"We've all got a kink inside of us. Me, I like screwing guys that are bad for me."

"No married jerks yet?" she asked.

"I didn't know that bastard was married, Martha. I did tell you."

Straight out of high school Lynne started dating a guy at the law practice where she was a temp worker. She got involved with the guy only to find out eight weeks later that the guy was married with three kids. At the time Lynne had been unaware the guy had a reputation for testing out the temps, and breaking them in to be used.

Martha didn't even want to know how a woman could go that long without finding out the truth. She believed Lynne, though.

"Anyway, you're keeping out of trouble?" Martha asked.

"I'm out of trouble. I told you I'm working hard to make my name in the law firm. There's no time for trouble when everyone is staring at you."

Martha nodded. "I get it."

Lynne parked up at the bar, making sure Martha wouldn't have any trouble when they left later that night. Checking the time, Martha saw it was past six. She was hungry, and she really didn't want to sit at a bar for the rest of the night, but it was something her friend wanted. She'd cancelled on Lynne before, and she wasn't surprised that Lynne had finally come to her.

They entered the town bar, and Martha took a seat toward the back. The bar was busy but not too crowded. By the end of the night it would be busy, and a fight would probably break out.

"I'm hungry," Martha said.

"I don't think they come to the tables to order food."

"That's no good. I need food now. What do you want?"

Lynne told Martha what she wanted, and Martha

made her way toward the bar to make an order. She leaned against the bar, tapping her fingers against the counter. Martha was minding her own business, waiting for her order to be taken when suddenly, the hairs on the back of her neck stood on end, and she turned.

The moment she saw him, Martha went back two years to inside the rehabilitation center moments after Becky had shouted at her. It didn't matter how many months had passed, or what had happened since. They were staring at each other from across the room, and she would have recognized him anywhere.

"Teddy," she said.

"Hello, Martha."

She let out a little squeal, and rushed toward him. It had been too long, and when Teddy had been leaving the rehab center, he'd been a lot thinner than he was now. He'd filled out a lot in the last two years. He picked her up, twirling her on the spot, chuckling.

Hearing him chuckle had goosebumps erupting all over her arms. It was a good sound, and not one she was actually used to.

When he put her down, she held onto his shoulders, not wanting him to leave, and trying to convince herself that he was actually real.

"I can't believe it's you. You're standing here, right now, in my arms." She laughed, unable to believe what she was seeing.

"I'm here, in the living flesh."

She touched his cheek, and then ran her hand down his chest. "What are you doing here?"

"I needed to get away from the club for a little bit. I remember what you said about coming to see you, and I figured I'd take you up on that offer. You didn't give me a timeline for how long it could be for me to visit."

"I didn't give you a date or how long the offer was on the table, but that was over two years ago. You still got my address after all this time?"

"Yes. Do you still have mine?"

"No, Becky tore it up. I wanted to reach out to you, but then I didn't want you to remember the pain you went through during rehab. I stayed away hoping you'd be happy. I can't believe you're here. It's surreal."

"I still go by Dick, and yes, I'm here."

"How long?"

"For however long you can handle me."

"You're not that bad a guy, Dick. I know you pretend to be, but you're not fooling me. When were you coming to find me?"

"I was coming to your place when I got hungry. Saw this bar, and stopped by for a bite to eat. Once I was done, I was going to stop by."

"I'm just ordering some food. Would you like to sit with me and Lynne? She's my friend, over there." She pointed toward the back of the room.

"Sure."

They both turned back to the bar, and Martha couldn't stop smiling. He'd made it. Dick had made it through for two years, and he was still clean. Her time hadn't been wasted, and he was here. She didn't want to over-think her response to him. She couldn't stop smiling though. He really was here.

Chapter Three

Dick followed Martha back to her table, and couldn't get over how beautiful she was. He'd always thought she was beautiful, but seeing her now, he was shocked by how much he'd actually missed of her beauty while in rehab. Her smile still enthralled him, and he didn't want to look away for fear of missing it. She really called to him, like a moth was called to a flame. He was the moth, and she the flame. During those months he'd not paid attention to anything other than the pain and need overriding his body. He'd wanted to deal with the reason why he was there, not think about anyone else.

"Lynne, this is Teddy, but he prefers to be called Dick. He's from the rehab center where Becky was. Dick, this is my friend, Lynne."

Martha made the introductions, and Dick shook Lynne's hand. He made sure to sit next to Martha, and he wasn't interested in her friend.

"Dick?"

"It's my road name."

"Road name?"

"He's a biker. You're part of the Chaos Bleeds crew, right?"

"Yes."

"Wow, a real biker. Where's your leather cut?" Lynne asked.

He was bored with the woman in front of him. The last thing he wanted to do was talk to the bitch in front of him. He didn't leave his club behind for a break to get in touch with Martha just to start talking to another woman.

"Out of respect to any MCs that claim this territory, I don't wear a leather cut." He shot Lynne a glare, waiting for her to say some shit to him. When she stayed quiet, he nodded. Good, he didn't want her to keep up her questions. "How have you been?" He directed his question to Martha.

Her cheeks went a beautiful shade of red, which he found so adorable. He wanted to reach out and touch her, see if her skin was as soft as it looked. Dick couldn't believe the feelings that were overtaking him at simply being near her.

"Erm, I've been fine. I've been working hard, and dealing with my stuff. Gardening, attempting to grow all my own fruit and vegetables," Martha said.

"What about Becky? How is she handling her shit?" he asked. He'd never made an effort with women, and he was out of practice in getting women to talk. Becky was the last thing he wanted to talk about, but it was their joint connection, the rehab center. It would be rude to ignore her sister, wouldn't it? Did he even want Martha to talk about her sister, or about anything?

Yes, you do. It's why you're here. You want her to talk, and you want her to tell you everything about her.

"Becky's dead." This came from Lynne after Martha went silent.

"Dead?"

"She didn't handle rehab well. Erm, it was hard for her," Martha said.

"How long has she been dead?" He didn't take his gaze of Martha.

"She died two months after getting out of rehab, which would have been a month after you, I think." She tried her best to smile, but it didn't reach her eyes. Dick didn't like it. Martha should laugh, smile, be happy with life. He wanted to hurt everyone who'd put that pain in her eyes. "I need to go to the bathroom." Dick hated Becky. The cold heartless bitch had done nothing but cause her sister pain.

He moved out of the way so she could get past him to use the bathroom. Watching her leave, he took a seat, and returned his gaze to Lynne. "What happened?"

"You really want to know?"

"Yes."

Lynne let out a sigh. "This is eerie shit for me. She was thinking about you on the way over here, and suddenly you appear. I don't like it."

"I'm not here to cause Martha pain. I don't give a shit what you think. I like her. I came to see her. She helped me in rehab."

"I wish she could have helped Becky as well." Lynne rubbed at her temple. "She can't help anyone, and she wanted to."

"Tell me what happened."

Lynne licked her lips, leaning forward. "Martha took Becky home with her, but you and I both know Becky never got off the hard stuff. If you were inside the rehab center with her, you'd have seen the signs of Becky being high. She was a whore to the core, and could get whatever she wanted so long as she was prepared to suck the right cock, or fuck it."

"I know. I got my brothers to get it stopped. The guy who was supplying was dealt with, but if she wanted the hard stuff, Becky would have known the right people to ask."

"It didn't stop. Becky always found a way. The moment she was out of rehab, and in Martha's home, she went straight back to her pimp, and drug dealing boyfriend."

"What did she do?" Dick asked.

"Becky started working the streets in the city, and in this town. She made Martha's life a misery with her constantly bailing Becky out. I told her to just leave Becky alone, to kick her out. Martha wouldn't have any of it. I guess it's what makes her a better person than most. One night Martha gets a call from Becky. Her sister was scared, and Martha being Martha, went and got her. A word of warning to you, she knows how to handle a gun. Her father made sure both of his daughters could handle themselves."

"Then why the fuck was Martha going after her sister rather than the father?" Dick asked.

"Martha's parents are both dead. They were at the bank when it was being robbed. Her father tried to stop it and got shot for his trouble. When her mother tried to help her husband, she got shot. They were left to bleed out."

"Fucking hell."

"Like I said, she's not had her life easy. In fact I'd go so far as to say she's had it shit."

Dick ran a hand over his face. "Go on, tell me the rest."

"Martha got Becky out, but she got hit a few times for her trouble. It was only when she threatened the men with her gun, and fired did they take her seriously. I was on my way as well. She'd called me to help." Lynne tucked some hair behind her ears. "Becky shot up in the back of the car, trying to deal with her nerves. Bitch was selfish, and she didn't care for Martha no matter what she did. Martha got distracted, and curved off a ditch, hitting a tree."

His heart raced at the thought of Martha struggling for her life with her sister in the back, useless from her high.

"Becky OD'ed in the back of the car. With the way the car hit the tree, Martha ended up impaled on the chair. A branch through her leg, keeping her in place. She got torn up pretty bad. With her stuck in place, she couldn't turn her sister or get Becky to listen. Martha had to watch while her sister choked on her own vomit in the back of the car. Screaming, crying, and begging for help."

There really were no words. He couldn't think of a single thing to say.

"Martha almost died from blood loss. The fire crew had to cut her out of the car. Becky was pronounced dead on the scene. It was a mess."

"Hey, I'm back," Martha said.

Behind her was the waiter, handing them all their food. Dick had lost his appetite, but he wasn't going to make Martha paranoid. He started eating his fries, even though he wasn't hungry. Lynne didn't say another word, and he knew Martha wouldn't have wanted him to know everything. How Martha was finding reasons to smile was beyond him. She was a strong woman, the perfect woman who'd been given hard knocks in life.

"If you two don't mind. I'm going to head onto the dance floor, and try to find a man to dance with me," Lynne said. She'd finished her food, and Dick was more than happy to have her gone.

"I'm sorry about my friend. Lynne can be blunt."

"Don't forget that I can give as good as I get," he said, giving her a wink. "I'm not a dick for nothing."

Martha laughed. "So, you've been clean?"

"Yes. I've not shot up. I was tempted to cover my scars, but I wanted to see them, to know what I've been through." He lifted the sleeve of his shirt up, to show her.

She ran her hands over the marks. "I'm so proud of you, Dick."

"I like you, Martha. You can call me Teddy."

"Not Teddy Bear?"

"No, not Teddy Bear. You can call me Teddy, that's it, or Ted."

She chuckled, resting her head on his arm. "I

can't believe you're here."

"I know. It's nice."

"It is nice. I can talk to you about anything."

He kissed the back of her head. It was the most natural thing in the world for him. "It has been a long couple of years, for me, and for you."

"I take it Lynne brought you up to speed on all the crap that has happened in my life?"

"I know what you've been through."

"It's not that bad, not really," she said.

"Watching your sister choking until she died, that is a big deal. Don't try to pretend it's not. You're not fooling me."

She tensed up in his arms.

Dick didn't like it, and so he stepped out of the booth, offering his hand. "Come on, we need to go on that dance floor, and to dance. This is not a night for us to go over old worries. What is in the past, stays in the past."

"You don't dance."

"I'll dance to make your night." He led the way, keeping her close. Lynne was wrapped around another man, but Dick wasn't paying her any attention. He focused on Martha, bringing her in close to his body. Her curves molded against him as if that was where she was always supposed to be. This was what he wanted, and what Lydia couldn't give him.

She placed one of her hands on his shoulder while the other took his hand. "I'm surprised you know how to dance?"

"I know how to dance. I just don't like doing it."

"Why?"

"Some bitches think the wrong thing the moment you're dancing with them."

"You're not afraid of me thinking the wrong

thing?"

"No. You know the score."

"Even assholes deserve to dance every now and again," Martha said. "Why couldn't your road name have been asshole?"

"I'm a dick, baby, not an asshole." He pulled her in close when the music turned down. It felt so good having her in his arms. He didn't want to let her go, not ever.

"Where are you staying?"

"I don't know. I needed to get away from the club. A lot of shit has happened since I got out."

"You make it sound like jail."

"It was in a way. I couldn't get away. One of the old ladies in the club almost died a few months ago. She had pre-eclampsia. We saved her from a pimp when we first moved to Piston County."

"Piston County, that's right. I completely forgot where you were otherwise I'd have reached out to you. I couldn't remember. I'm so sorry."

He chuckled. "Let's just say there is a lot going on, and I needed a break. You were the one I thought about. No one else. I didn't even want to be alone."

"I'm glad."

"I'm glad that I came here as well. This is nice."

"If you need somewhere to stay, you can stay with me."

"Are you sure?" he asked. "I don't want to impose."

"You've come to stay with me. The least I can do is put you in a room. It will give us a chance to catch up, and you can tell me all about yourself."

****

Dick stayed in the back of the car while Lynne stared out of the window. It had been a good night.

Lynne had danced with pretty much every single guy who looked her way, and Martha had danced with Dick.

She pulled up outside of her home, and walked in.

"I'll take you on a tour tomorrow," Martha said.

"It's okay. I'll take a seat in the living room."

She nodded, giving him a big smile. Lynne had already made her way upstairs, the moment they walked into her home. Martha found Lynne in one of the spare bedrooms. She was already naked and making her way into the bathroom. Following her friend in, she watched as Lynne washed her face.

"You like him, don't you?"

"Yes, I like him."

"No, I mean, you like him, like him."

"I do. He was always kind to me in the rehab center." Martha tucked some hair behind her ear. "It's more than that. He's hurting inside. I see it in the way he looks at me. I know you don't like him."

"I don't know him. I don't know if he's even got a likeable bone in his body."

"It sucks, I know that. I like him, though."

"He's part of a life you wanted Becky to have, Martha. He's a biker, and he's used to having a lot of women. Be careful, and don't put yourself out for this man." Lynne pulled on a shirt. "Think about it."

"I have, and I will. I'm not going to allow myself to get hurt, and regardless of what you think, Dick's a good guy."

"Good. Now, I'm going to go to sleep." Lynne pulled her in for a hug. "I only talk so much because I get afraid for you."

"I love you, too."

Martha went to her own room, putting on a pair of pajama bottoms, and a shirt. She made her way downstairs to find Dick, or Teddy, sitting in one of the living room chairs. He was staring down at one of the family pictures of her, Becky, and their parents.

"Hey," she said.

"Lynne's worried about you," he said.

"You're the first person I've gotten close to in the last couple of years."

"You cut everyone out?" He placed the picture frame back on the table beside him.

"It was hard to be friends with people who kept calling your sister a whore. Becky had a lot of problems, but she was still my sister, and I loved her." Martha had cut off the pain and the fear, dealing with herself, on her own. "I went to the bank once and the guy behind the counter asked me if I was anything like my sister. He offered to give me extra so long as I was willing to give him extra."

"What did you do?" he asked.

"I went to his manager, got him fired. I made everyone who tried to make that mistake regret it. I wasn't going to be treated like shit just because my sister liked to." She moved to sit on the sofa opposite him. "Our father told us to stand up for what we wanted, and for what we believed in. I did that every day. Becky, she wanted a life filled with highs, and to make her life easy."

Biting her lip, Martha stared down at her crossed legs.

"You shouldn't have to fight to be seen as yourself."

She rested her hands on her knees smiling at him. "The world tends to paint a picture of you in ways you're not prepared to deal with."

"I get that."

"What about you? How are you handling it?"

He stared down at his arms. For a split second she

was sure she saw shame fill his gaze. It must have been in her head because he didn't say or do anything.

"In the beginning, I hated it. All I wanted to do was shoot up, get high, and just forget about the fucking world. You know I'm part of a biker club. Before we settled down in Piston County, we did whatever the fuck we wanted. Some of the brothers, they would smoke a bit of weed, shoot up, and it didn't affect them. Some of us, we got addicted, and it was our life. We still wore the patch, and we did our shit for the club. Life faded away." Dick ran a hand down his face. "As a club, we made a fucking big enemy. I'm talking the kind of enemy that can make it difficult for you to piss for two seconds in peace because he was always there. He showed us his power, and we were fucking helpless. Our women, the old ladies, they suffered because of it. Another club, The Skulls, they got hurt real bad as well. It was the worst time I can ever recall for us."

She listened to him pour out his soul. There was no other way to describe it. He was opening up to her. Martha wondered if he talked this openly with anyone else.

"Devil, our club president, he didn't like the balance of power out of our hands. He couldn't handle any of us being in prison on possession charges. All of the brothers who were addicts were admitted to rehab. He placed us in different rehab centers. Devil figured if we were all in the same center, we'd find a way to get shit there. He was probably right."

"You were all split apart."

"Yes. It was for the best. We were split apart, and while they were dealing with Gonzalez and all the crap that bastard was putting them through, we were getting clean. Some of us couldn't handle it though."

"Are you pleased you're clean?"

"I am. I mean, there are times I wish I wasn't. When reality gets too much I just want to shoot up, and forget about the shit."

"It numbs you?" she asked.

"Yeah. I don't have to care about anyone or anything. It makes me sound like a selfish bastard, but it's the truth. Caring puts everyone in danger, and it causes so much pain."

Martha sighed. "I know what you mean. I cared so much about Becky. She didn't give a shit about me. Dad put me in charge of our trust fund, and so Becky had to always come to me. She hated that."

"If she got her hands on money, she'd have put it into her veins."

"Yeah, she hated that as well. I always denied her requests for large amounts of money. Our friendship was strained for a long time, even before she went to rehab."

Dick moved out of the chair, and took a seat beside her. He tugged her into his arms. "I'm sorry you had to witness her choking like that."

Martha took an unsteady breath in. It was too much. She'd promised herself she wouldn't cry. She shouldn't cry. "I feel so guilty," she said.

"Why?"

"I hated her. I hated the way she left me. I hated the fact she made me lie like that. I fucking hated what she did to herself. She didn't need to do drugs, and yet she did, destroying herself. Why fuck assholes for money or drugs? Why?"

"Drugs make you do unspeakable things, baby."

"She didn't need to. They've all left me, Teddy. Mom, Dad, and Becky. They've all left me, and I'm so scared to love anyone or to let anyone in. They're only going to hurt me. I can't handle that. I don't want to handle that."

Her tears began to fall, and Teddy held her tightly. She didn't want to think of him as Dick. He was Teddy.

"No one is going to hurt you, baby. I won't let them. I'll be here. I'll always be here to keep an eye on you." He kissed the top of her head, and for some reason this just made her cry even more.

After several minutes had passed, she wiped at her nose, feeling a little worse for wear.

"I can't believe I'm crying at you."

"You don't need to worry about anything, baby. You don't need to worry about crying."

"Wow, I thought you were supposed to be a dick," she said. "You're being incredibly sweet, and I can't get upset with you if you're being sweet."

He chuckled.

"Do you think that's why she's gone? Because I got so angry with her for doing what she did?" Martha asked.

"No. I think she's gone because she kept testing the limits of her own control. Drugs are not the answer. That was what I realized in rehab. It didn't matter how much I took, it never helped. I was still clueless at the end of the high, only time had passed."

"Is that what your time in rehab taught you?" she asked, glancing up at him.

"No. It's what you taught me. Everything else I've realized on my own. Rehab was just a building that kept me safe while the drugs were out of my system."

"Wow, I sound like an awesome person right now, and rehabs sound awful."

"You are awesome, and rehabs only work for people who want to get clean." He cupped the back of her head, and for a split second she was sure he was going to kiss her. Suddenly he stopped and released her.

Martha didn't know what to do, and so she pulled away. "I'm going to go and make up your spare room."

Tapping his thigh, she got to her feet, and made her way upstairs. She'd wanted him to kiss her, and yet he'd not. What had she done wrong?

You're the girl he remembers from rehab.

This isn't about getting together.

It's about providing him with a break.

She kept cursing herself, over and over, to make sure she understood that what was happening between them wasn't down to anything but the fact he wanted a break. She wasn't special, nor was she different.

You're the girl with the dead drug addict sister. He probably feels nothing but pity for you.

"Are you all right?" he asked, leaning against the doorframe. He looked so damn good, and Martha just smiled.

"Yes, I'm fine. Erm, does your club know where you are?"

"They know I needed to take a break. Don't worry, none of us are going to swarm down on you, and start hurting your place or anything."

She smiled. "I wouldn't worry about that." Martha would have gotten each of them to do some work. "Everything is ready. I hope you have a good night's sleep."

Dick reached out, grabbing her arm.

She stared up at him.

"What is it?" she asked.

"I locked up the house."

"You don't need to lock up the house. It's perfectly safe."

"Then bad shit happens to women like you. Don't leave your house unlocked again."

Martha pulled out of his hold and made her way

toward her own room. She closed the door, leaning against it. Pressing a hand to her neck, she felt her rapidly beating pulse, and couldn't help licking her lips. He'd turned her on, aroused her, and now she was panting for more. She'd liked the way he touched her. He had to have cared about her in some way to tell her to lock up her house.

Touching between her thighs, she stifled a moan.

What had Dick done to her?

****

Spider watched as Beauty danced in front of the audience. Naked Fantasies was thriving with activity for a Friday night. He glanced around at the men staring at his woman on the stage. Paris, or Beauty as everyone knew her as, was his. Sure, she couldn't stand to be around him, but he really didn't give a fuck.

He'd taken her home the other day, and he was shocked to find her living in a decent home. It was in one of the nicest areas of town, and yet she was stripping. She'd strut on stage, and the music would start. Beauty knew how to keep the audience on her with each swift sway of her hips.

She hypnotized the crowd, and made them believe that they were the ones responsible for her still being semi-clothed by the end of her set. He loved it, and when the club had received complaints, Spider had been the one to deal with it. Spider had given Paris a warning, so she'd worked other elements into her routine. She teased, and tantalized the men with views of her tits, making them beg for more. She was the mistress on the stage, and she knew how to work the crowd. Beauty was one of the most requested dancers, and the men panted for more of her. Providing Paris gave the club what was in the contract, they kept the customers happy, and at bay. Some of the girls were pretty much so desperate by the end of their set that they were practically fucking the customers. Beauty knew her music. She knew how to make it last and how to give a brilliant performance.

"What's going on?" Butler asked, taking a seat at their table.

Several of the brothers were in tonight to blow off steam. They were dotted around the club, each giving the other the space they required. The married men of their club were nowhere to be seen. They didn't need to come to the club to let off steam.

Devil never came to the strip club unless he had to lay down the law. "No drugs" was still a firm Chaos Bleeds rule. At times Spider believed he'd grown soft since being married to Lexie. Now, he didn't believe it at all. The man was a hard fucker, and had gotten harder with Lexie. He was a fucking lion protecting his family.

"They're all watching her," he said, staring at the woman on stage. This was her last set of the night. Spider hadn't even touched any of his drink. He didn't want to. She'd flashed her tits to the men on the left, and given everyone her back, teasing them with what she had on show. Beauty was like another woman. He wanted to climb up onto the stage, and grab her ass, pushing her forward and fucking her hard.

"Damn, man. She's paid to strip. The bitch is doing her job."

"Don't call her that."

"What do you want me to call her? Pussy?" Butler shook his head. "Don't get involved."

"Something's not right with her."

"Why? She's stripping to some men, but not to others, and something isn't right for you?"

Spider tapped his fingers on the counter as the set ended. "I've got to find out what the fuck is going on."

He threw down some notes, and made his way

outside. Moving around to the back, he watched the door for her to exit. It took several minutes before Paris was outside. The moment she spotted him, her shoulders slumped. If he had a problem with his ego, her reaction to him would affect him. As it was, Spider was very happy with himself.

"Have I done something wrong? Is this a club thing of warning me that I've done something wrong? I changed my routine like you told me. I'm teasing the crowd with exposing my body. Do you need more?"

"No."

"Then what's going on?"

"Nothing. It's a new kind of service. I'm taking you home."

"I don't know you."

"You know me."

"Knowing your name isn't a good thing. I don't know who you are. I don't know what you're capable of, and right now, you're freaking me out. This is verging on major stalker." She hiked her bag high on her shoulder.

"You're a dancer."

"No."

"You are. There's no way an amateur dances the way you do. You know how to work a crowd."

She shook her head, looking down the street. "Will you just leave me alone?"

"What are you hiding?"

"I'm not hiding anything."

She started walking down the street, but Spider wasn't done. He grabbed her arm, turning her so that she had no choice but to face him.

"I'm not going to back down," he said. "I'm going to find out the truth."

"Whatever. There is no truth to find out. It's late, and I'm tired."

Spider didn't let her go. Paris was going to learn the hard way that when he wanted something, there was no getting away from him.

"I'll give you a ride home."

He'd find out his answers, and when he knew what was going on, he'd put a stop to whatever bad shit was happening in her life.

Chapter Four

At six in the morning Dick was awake, making himself a cup of coffee, and sitting on the back porch overlooking the large property that Martha owned. It was beautiful, and he sat watching the sun come up, enhancing the beauty before him. Ever since he'd gotten off the drugs, and become sober, he'd been an early riser. There was nothing keeping him in bed, and he'd found there were moments while watching the sunrise that he found a kind of peace that was usually rather foreign to him.

The drugs were the things that kept him in bed, while having a clear mind kept him alert.

"I didn't expect you to be up," Lynne said, coming outside. "I thought bikers were supposed to be lazy, spending most of their time in bed."

She was dressed in a pair of pajamas with a blanket wrapped around her.

"I don't sleep late, and not all bikers are the same."

"That's good to know. I'll change my views that all bikers are damn lazy. I suppose it's good for Martha, you being an early riser."

"You don't need to worry about Martha. I'm not the lazy kind of biker, not anymore. You're a lawyer. Shouldn't you be impartial or something?"

"I'm not on the clock. I can be whatever the hell I want to be. Now, if this was a business meeting, I'd be different."

"I'm pleased you're not one of my lawyers."

"You couldn't afford me."

Dick smirked. Chaos Bleeds could afford the best lawyers in the state, but he wasn't about to tell her that. He didn't like her, and the club already had a lawyer.

There was no way Lynne would ever get the job. Devil would chew her up and spit her back out.

Taking a sip of his coffee, he stared straight ahead of him.

"What are you doing out here?" Lynne asked.

"I don't see how that's any of your business."

"It's not. Martha, she's my business. We're best friends, and she concerns me."

"I'm not going to hurt her."

"You are. You may not think you're going to hurt her, but somewhere down the line, you're going to unintentionally hurt her. I can't let that happen, so you need to move on. She's been through enough."

Gritting his teeth, Dick stared at the woman. "I'm not going anywhere, and you're not going to scare me away." He talked slowly so she knew he wasn't joking around.

"Martha has been hurt enough. She lives her life as a recluse, sticking close to the home her parents started up, leaving the world behind. I'm trying to get her out of here. I'm trying to—"

"You're trying to change her. I'm not here to change her. I'm here to spend time with her. You're the one that's in the fucking wrong. So she likes spending time with fucking plants, big deal. She's been through enough shit that when *she's* ready to join the real world, she will. Believe me, that crap out there is waiting for her. It will suck her up, and tear her inside fucking out. She'll know within minutes what's going on. You're pushing her, and you need to give her time."

"You don't understand."

"No. I understand perfectly. *You* don't understand. You think you're being the good friend, getting her to leave this place, to go on dates. What happens when that shit messes up, huh? What happens if the guy she meets beats the shit out of her, and takes this one safe place that she's got in the world, and destroys that? You ever thought about the evil shit you're about to expose her to?"

"I wouldn—"

"You may be a big hot-shot lawyer, but the truth is, you don't know shit. You don't know shit about the world we live in. You're pure whereas Martha's had all the knocks. You can look in, and pretend you know what is going on, but you can't tell her how to live her life. You're an outsider to the pain."

He took another sip of his coffee. Any ordinary person would have stormed away from Lynne. Dick wasn't like that. He liked to antagonize, to force people to face their own truth.

"I'm trying to help her."

"If you were really her friend, you'd see the only help she required was that of fucking support. You want to get fucked, go out, and find your own dick to satisfy your cunt. Don't use her to get what you want."

"I wasn't doing that."

"No, then where are your other friends, huh? Where are you perfect business buddies that you rub shoulders with all through the fucking week?"

She went to speak, and he made a noise that was verging on disgust. This was what he hated about the world he lived in. People really believed they had a right to tell someone else how to live their life. It wasn't up to anyone else, not him, not the government, no one. Martha had been hurt, and the way she was dealing with that hurt was to place herself at home, away from it all.

He knew what that was like. Dick could relate to Martha, and he understood. Staring out over the sunrise, he saw the freedom that she was living. There was nothing holding her down right now. The outside world was scary as fuck, and it was full of pain and hate. Martha hiding away was her way of dealing. Every time she'd been out, people had hurt her. This way, she didn't suffer any pain or heartache.

"I fucking hate people like you. You're all the same. If someone is fine, and not living to your fucking social model, you try to change it. Martha is fine. She's dealing with her shit in her own way. You shouldn't force her to be like you. She's not like you, and if she was, she'd be out there in the city, rubbing shoulders with you. She's a big girl, an intelligent one."

"You really do care about her?" Lynne asked.

Dick turned to see tears in her eyes. He didn't respond. Her tears did nothing for him. Last night when Martha was crying in his arms, he'd been torn up. He'd wanted to hurt the sister, and every single person who'd taken a shot at her. He wanted to hurt them all, to let them know that Martha was protected, and no one was ever going to hurt her again.

They fell silent, and Dick wasn't about to break that silence. He hated it when his morning was interrupted. Once he finished his coffee, he made his way inside, and froze. Martha was stood in the kitchen, making her own drink. The way she looked at him made him aware that she'd heard everything that he'd said.

"Morning," she said.

Lynne came into the kitchen after him. "Hey, sweetie. I've got to head out. Did you have a good night?"

He waited to see if Martha would say anything. She didn't. He watched as she hugged her friend, and chatted about the night. Leaning against the counter, he was intrigued, and he needed to know what the hell was going on with Martha. Why wasn't she cursing at them?

When they were alone, he leaned against the

counter, and waited.

Martha took her time stirring her coffee. Every now and then she'd glance over at him.

"What?" she asked, finally speaking up.

"You heard our argument."

"It was hard not to hear it. You were both shouting at the tops of your voice. I thought my head was going to literally explode. You're not exactly considerate to the early morning risers." She placed her hands by either side of her head and made a crash sound.

"Why didn't you say anything?"

"What would have been the point? You were both fighting about nothing."

"We were fighting about you."

"Yeah, I don't really care."

She took her coffee and made her way outside.

"I don't know what to make of this. What the hell is going on?" he asked.

"What's going on is I'm drinking my coffee, and enjoying the last of the sunrise. I slept in, and I don't usually sleep in." She took a sip of her coffee, and Dick couldn't look away from her. "I'm not going to change who I am. What you said to Lynne was fine to me. I'm happy living in this small little world. I'm safe here, and no one can take that away from me. I'm happy."

He nodded. "You have a nice place."

"Yes," she said, sighing as she did.

"What was that?"

"You think it's beautiful. Wait until you see all the work that needs to be done?"

"Work?"

"Yeah. This isn't just any garden. This is my fruit and vegetable garden. I've got a set of new potatoes coming out today. I've also got to take the ripe tomatoes so they don't rot, pick up carrots, water, feed, et cetera.

It's going to be busy. You sure you can handle it?"

He chuckled. "If you can handle it, I can. Let me go and get changed. I'll help you out."

Dick kissed the top of her head, and made his way inside. He passed Lynne, who grabbed his arm.

"What?" he asked. He wasn't interested in getting into another argument.

"I'm pleased you're here for her. She needs someone who cares about her."

"I do care about her." He really did. Martha was the first person outside of his club that he cared about.

He pulled away from her touch, and made his way to his room. Pulling out his cell phone, he dialed Butler.

"What's up?" Butler asked, sounding alert.

"I was just letting you know I arrived, and I'm fine."

"Yeah, Devil said you'd be calling to give an update."

"How is everything back home?" Dick asked.

"You've been gone a little over a day, and you're wanting to know how everything is?" Dick didn't say anything. There wasn't any need for him to speak. "Everything is more than fine here. Really, you don't need to worry about a thing. Judi, Ripper, and Paul are fine. The club's fine. Lexie and the new baby are fine. We're all fine. Apart from Spider. He's been in a mood for too damn long, and he's pissing me off."

Dick shook his head. "I'm just giving everyone the heads-up. I don't need a breakdown of how everyone is at the club." It would take too damn long.

"We're aware you're still alive."

"Bye."

He hung up the phone, and then put a call through to Spider. His curiosity was getting the better of him.

Spider was usually the easygoing guy who didn't have a problem with anyone or anything, and yet, he was being told differently.

When Spider answered the phone, he mumbled out his response.

"What's going on with you?" Dick asked.

"Dick, you're supposed to be having a break, and you're calling my ass right now?" There was some commotion in the background, and Spider growled. "You're calling me at six-thirty, you fucking asshole. I got in late last night. You're doing this to piss me off."

He smirked. Spider had never been much of a morning person. It was one of the reasons he was the better option for sticking around the strip club. He'd be awake until the early hours of the morning. Spider probably didn't get to bed until three.

"It's that early? Really? I didn't know."

"You're a fucking asshole. I fucking hate you right now."

"Well, spill what crap you've got going on. You're up, so you may as well tell me."

"Fuck off."

Spider hung up on him. There was no point in calling him back. Spider would only smash the phone, and that wouldn't do either of them any good. He put the phone down, laughing as he did.

Getting dressed, Dick suddenly stopped. For the first time in over five years, he'd laughed, and it had felt good. It wasn't a forced laugh. He was actually happy. In that moment, Dick couldn't remember a time when he'd been happy. Getting away from the club had been a good idea. He was, in fact, happy.

****

Martha was developing a huge crush on Dick. When he'd been in the rehab center, she'd found him attractive, but he'd been a patient, someone to care for. Now, with his shirt removed and sweat glistening on his body. He looked hot, sexy hot. Any thought of him being a patient who needed help had disappeared. She licked her lips, imagining licking the sweat from his body. Ew, what was wrong with her? Dick made sweat look good.

She ducked her head, and pulled up the latest weeds in her late potato bed.

Focus, Martha, focus.

The job she was currently doing would usually only take her a couple of minutes to get done. With Dick distracting her, she couldn't focus on anything but him. He was driving her crazy, and she was turned on. Working on potatoes while being aroused wasn't good. When did a woman get horny while gardening? Okay, so not many women had a hot man like Dick close, but she wasn't a teenager. She had control over her urges and needs. This was not something she suffered with. It had been a good two years since she'd been turned on, maybe even longer. There was a short time she believed her pussy had stopped working because she didn't get aroused anymore.

She didn't know whether to be happy or sad that her body was suddenly waking up, letting her know she was in fact alive. For the longest time she'd forgotten what it meant to be a woman. She was the good daughter, the good sister, the doormat, or the whore's sister. There had never been a chance where she could literally be herself. Dick wasn't expecting her to be anyone else, or pretend. He wanted her to be herself, and it really was refreshing.

He mowed her lawn, and she found herself watching him more than she was watching what she was doing. Dick stopped, wiped at his brow, glanced her way, and smiled.

"You like what you see?"

"Yes." Heat filled her cheeks, and she started to stutter. Dick didn't help matters by sauntering over to her. His arms still held the old track marks. She'd recognize them anywhere, but she didn't find them repulsive. They showed the kind of man he was, a fighter to the core. They were a sign of the battle that he had in life. "Erm, it's a little hot. I've, erm, I've got to get some drink."

She placed her trowel in the ground and stood. Dusting the mud off her hands, she moved around him, not trusting herself to be near him, or to touch him. She wasn't used to feeling this lack of control. Was his skin hot to the touch from the sun beating down? This was completely out of her comfort zone. Keeping her head bent down, she rushed into her kitchen. Seconds later she heard the lawn mower start up. Taking a deep breath, she rested against the counter, and tried to think of sheep, or something that would cool her body off.

Staring out of the window, she watched his back move over her lawn.

"He's just a guy. There's nothing going on here. It's nothing. He's just a guy, a friend. A sexy, hot, really great friend. Stop it, Martha. He's not here for that. Focus."

It wasn't nothing, she knew that.

When Dick had been in rehab she'd grown attached to him, enjoying his company far more than anyone else. Becky had once accused her of using the center to pick up men. She hadn't, but she would look forward to seeing him. Dick had been the highlight of her visits. He didn't call her names, shout, or curse her. He made her feel welcome when that should have been Becky's job. Her sister never appreciated her visits, so there was no point in trying too hard for Becky. She'd tried for Dick.

I'm a horrible person.

What kind of person tried harder for a man she barely knew? He always seemed to enjoy her visits while Becky just complained. She would complain about the heat, the lack of comfort, the food, the men, the lack of money. Everything Beck could find to complain about, she did.

Pouring out two large sweet teas, Martha walked back out.

Dick stopped mowing the lawn and moved to her side.

"So are you seeing anyone else? Anything casual?" he asked.

"No. There's no one. I mean, the postman comes throughout the week, but there's nothing going on there. I'm alone here. I like the quiet."

"When was the last time you dated someone?"

"Are you asking me out on a date?"

Dick tilted his head to the side. "I'm not."

"Of course you're not. I mean, we barely know each other."

"It's not because of that. We know each other. We know more about each other than most people would in a lifetime."

"That's true, but it has been two years since we've seen each other. A lot can happen in that time."

"I don't care about the time between. We know each other where it matters most."

She took a deep breath, barely believing what she was hearing. "It's a long time. People change."

"I've changed, Martha. I'm not the same man I was in the rehab center. I'm clean. I'm sober, and at times I find that hard."

"Why?" she asked, staring up at him. It took

every single ounce of willpower not to stare at his body. He wasn't wearing a shirt, and it was hard for her not to look at his glorious body.

Dick was a handsome man. In the center, because of the withdrawal and drugs, he'd lost a lot of weight, too much. He'd been skin and bones. Now, he'd filled out in all the right places with muscles everywhere.

"Life is hard. It's hard, and it's painful, and it's so fucking unfair. I figure a high is worth it."

Her gut tightened. There was no other word to describe it. Becky had always been an adventurous person even when they were growing up. She'd wanted to try everything, to be everything. The life and soul of the party, but it all came with consequences.

"So you get high for a few hours, but the thing is, everything stays the same."

"What do you mean?"

"Getting high doesn't take the problem away. You get high, waste the hours it's taken to forget about the problem, only it's still there. Becky, she got high when our parents died, and after her high and forgetting everything, they were still dead."

"I'm not trying to condone—"

She held her hand up. "I know you're not trying to condone or even take her side. I'm telling you the way I see it. I suffered right along with my sister. I didn't do drugs. I didn't drink. I faced everything head on. I acknowledged our parents' deaths. I dealt with it. Becky, she would always come down, and the facts would remain the same. Our parents were still dead, and each time she came back to reality, she hated it. That's not dealing with anything, or even getting high. It's trying to escape something that can't be escaped from."

"I never thought about it like that."

"I dealt with my parents' deaths. It took me a

couple of months to accept it, and over time, it got a little easier. Becky ignored the truth, and so she suffered all the time. She couldn't handle what was right in front of her." Martha took a sip of her drink. She thought she'd be close to tears, but she wasn't. The time for mourning had passed for her. She had accepted what had happened, moved on, and dealt with it. Becky had thought she was heartless as she stopped crying. Her sister was never there for Martha in the beginning when she did cry all the time. She'd be standing in the kitchen, grab a wooden spoon, and sob remembering her mother's cooking.

No, she wasn't heartless. She simply didn't run away like everyone else.

Crying was the last thing she wanted to do.

"Getting high is a waste of time?" he asked.

She chuckled. "It doesn't exactly help. What are you trying to get away from?"

Dick looked away. "You're the first woman to ever ask that."

"Is there someone back home?"

"No."

"You don't sound too sure about that."

"I thought I was with someone, and I can't stand her. I was only helping her out. I thought she was the kind of woman I deserved."

Jealousy struck Martha hard. "Deserved?" She hoped he didn't detect the bitterness in her voice.

"I'm not a good man, Martha. I've never done good things. There are things I'm not even proud of. I guess I figured if I was that ashamed of what I'd done, I didn't deserve any kind of real happiness."

"So you're punishing yourself by being with a woman you can't stand?" Martha asked.

"No. One of my brothers already took care of the talk for me. He told me that I deserved to have as much happiness as I wanted."

"Brothers? I didn't know you had a family."

"I don't. The club I'm with. That's my family. They're the guys that will always have my back."

"You sound very close together. It must be nice."

"They're the only family I've got. Yeah, they drive me fucking crazy, but then, that's life."

"Yeah, that's life. We win some, we lose some."

He looked so sad. Closing the distance between them, she wrapped her arms around him, keeping him close. It wasn't about sex for her. She wanted to offer him comfort.

Dick wrapped his arms around her, holding her close. Martha closed her eyes, inhaling his scent. He was the first man she'd been close to. It had been well over three years since she'd been with anyone. With Becky, men gravitated to her sister more than her. Martha had not minded, or at least she'd tried not to care. Martha would introduce any boyfriends to Becky before she slept with them. They always ended up wanting Becky more than they wanted her, until Dick entered her life. He'd only been interested in her, and she'd liked that about him.

When his hand ran down the back of her shirt, the fabric was so light that it was almost as if he was touching her skin. She closed her eyes, licking her lips. Her body came to life at his touch, and she didn't want him to stop.

"What's the matter, Martha?" he asked.

His voice seemed husky as if he was feeling the tension as well.

"Nothing."

You're arousing me in ways a man never has before.

He moved his hand up to the back of her neck,

gripping just a little tighter. She gasped out at the pressure, and he pulled her closer. Dick leaned in while she stared at his lips. What would it be like to have those lips on hers, attacking hers, devouring her?

Martha wanted to know, she needed to know, and yet what would happen if it took their relationship to the next level, and they weren't ready for that?

It was as if he read her mind.

Dick pulled away, giving her a smile. "I better get this lawn finished so I can work on something else tomorrow."

Pushing away her disappointment, Martha simply nodded. "Sure."

She grabbed the two glasses of sweet tea and made her way inside the house.

"It was stupid to think he'd kiss me. Why would he? I'm a no one. A no one who has nothing to do with his club, or anyone else. I bet he has a lot of hot women at the club who'll be with him all the time. Here I am, talking to myself."

She washed the glasses before making her way outside. Forcing herself to not look at him, she went back to weeding through her plants even with the sun high in the sky. At some point Dick walked toward her, and placed a cap on her head. "Keeps the sun out."

They didn't speak to each other for the remainder of the day.

****

"Dick made it where he needed to go," Devil said, coming downstairs from putting the kids to bed. He was back home in the house that he'd bought for his family, close to his friend Vincent. Devil never thought he would settle down, be in love, and have a family of his own. He'd been on the road all of his life, growing his club, but it had happened, and he was grateful for it.

"Where did he go?" Lexie asked.

He followed her as she walked back into her kitchen, admiring the curves of her ass. She'd given birth to three of his children, and to him, her body was still as beautiful as the day he first met her, dancing on a pole. His love for Lexie had rivaled that of his club. She was everything to him. Lexie and the kids had become his world, and she'd embraced the club even though it scared the living hell out of him at times the danger she was in.

"I don't know. He needed to get away from the club, open his mind up, and I wasn't going to stop him. It's the first time he's come to me in a long time." He took a seat at the kitchen counter while the scent of baking permeated the air.

Lexie loved to bake, and he'd been taking more and more delicious items into the clubhouse with him daily.

"It's not like him to need a break from the club. Dick's usually the one driving people crazy."

"Dick has had it hard the last couple of years. He was always a great guy for the club. Stuck up for us, and all he did was do drugs. Sure, he hit the drugs hard, but he could always take a shot for a brother. He never had a problem risking his life for the club. I respect him."

Lexie moved away from the stove and placed a hand on his shoulder. "You shouldn't feel guilty for making your boys get clean. They shouldn't feel anything for you but being grateful to you. If you hadn't done it, they might have ended up in a worse place now."

"I promised them I wouldn't interfere with the way they ran their life. Chaos Bleeds was about no rules, and to respect the road."

"That was when there was no threat, but everything changed. You came to Piston County not just for your son, but to find a place to call your own. So you met me, and we got married. Things change. The club didn't change because of you, Devil. They changed because you had to keep your boys safe. There was an outside force here. Don't forget that."

No, he wasn't going to forget anything anytime soon. Gonzalez had taken a great deal from him, and yet, he'd given a great deal of his club their life back. If Devil hadn't sent them to rehab, they would have eventually ended up dead at some point.

"Whatever sent Dick away, he's dealing in his own way."

"I hope he's not using," Devil said.

He loved all of his men at Chaos Bleeds. There wasn't a single man that he wouldn't die for. It was what made Chaos Bleeds so deadly. They were a deadly wall, each brother willing to stand up, take a bullet, and fight for another day.

"Dick's many things, but his love for the club is never shaken, Devil. If he wanted to cheat the club, he wouldn't have gone to rehab, and he'd have left when you gave him the choice."

"He's a dick to the core."

Lexie chuckled. "I don't think he is. Sure, he pisses everyone off with his shitty attitude, but really, I believe it's a front. I don't think for a moment he's always honest with himself. He had to get away because of Lydia. He can't stand her. No one really likes her."

"The guys like that she is easy."

"Dick was going to take her as his old lady until he got his head out of his ass."

Devil had to admit that there was more to Dick than him riling people up, getting a rise out of them. "He deserves a good woman."

"He'll be good, and when he's ready, he'll come back to us. Hopefully with a much better woman than

Lydia."

Taking her hand, Devil pulled his woman down to his lap. "How long until this cake is done? I need to be inside you."

"It's already done. When did you start asking for permission?"

SAM CRESCENT

Chapter Five

After Dick almost kissed Martha, they'd gone to either end of the garden. He wanted to kiss her, and he didn't know what stopped him. She had looked a little uncertain about the kiss, and so he'd released her. He couldn't help but watch her every now and then, just because she was so beautiful, and he didn't want to look away. The woman, who was now picking strawberries, was nothing like Lydia. Personality, looks, or just general interests, they were nothing alike. Lydia was a selfish bitch who lost her friendship with Jessica. She liked to fuck, and that was about it. He couldn't find any other reason to like her, whereas he liked everything about Martha. He liked the way she smiled, the way she tucked her hair behind her ear, rubbing her forehead with the back of her hand. All of it was charming to him.

Martha held a variety of interests, and he'd seen some of those interests in the how-to books she had in abundance. She cared about her friend, and he didn't see Martha calling Lynne for a guy that was torturing her. Martha would be the kind of woman who'd die before letting any harm come to her friend.

Resting his chin on the rake, he simply admired her curvy ass. She filled out a pair of shorts to perfection. Even though he saw the outline of her panties, he found himself getting more aroused by the sight before him. She spun around, bent down, and he had to look away. The top gaped enough so that he saw the rounded globes of her tits.

Raking at some of the weeds, he kept working. If he didn't work, he was going to walk over there, and fuck her. There was no one around. They could fuck out in the open without fear of anyone looking at them. It would be so easy to. He was hard as fucking rock,

75

making it impossible to move around.

Minutes passed, he didn't know how many, when she finally came over.

"I've got a couple of steaks. Would you like them on the grill?" she asked.

"Sure, bring them out."

He wiped the sweat from his forehead, and made his way over to the grill. His cell phone started to buzz, and he answered without looking at the screen.

"Hello," he said.

"When are you coming back to the club?" Lydia asked.

Any arousal he had disappeared. Nothing like the reminder of his mistake to dampen his need for another. Why the fuck did he even think he'd be able to put up with that bitch? No one could handle Lydia long term. She was too needy, too bitchy. The list was endless.

"What do you want, Lydia?" he asked. He glanced toward the kitchen to find Martha still inside. He didn't want to have to explain Lydia to her.

"I'm bored. I'm needy, and I want you."

Closing his eyes, he rubbed at his temples. "I'm not coming home."

"Why not?"

Her whiny voice was starting to grate on his nerves.

"You do realize we're not an exclusive thing? I don't want you as my old lady. I did tell you this before I fucking left. Are you fucking thick? Do you need me to write it down on a piece of paper for you to understand?" He was losing his temper.

"I get the damn hint, you bastard."

"Do you? Why are you calling me? You can fuck whatever man you want. Your pussy doesn't belong to me. I don't want you."

"Fuck you, Dick. You weren't that good in bed anyway."

"I wasn't that good?" he asked, smirking.

"No, you weren't."

"Then why did you scream like a fucking banshee every time I fucked you? The only reason you're calling me now is no other man can give you what you want. Fuck you, Lydia, don't call me again."

Turning off his cell, he went back to the grill but caught sight of Martha holding a plate with the steaks on it. Her cheeks had gone pale, and she must have heard the phone call.

"I'm sorry about what you heard."

"It's nothing. I guess listening in on someone else's conversation gets you in all kinds of trouble. I thought you didn't have a girlfriend?"

"It's not what it looked like, and I don't have a girlfriend."

She handed him the steaks. "It's no way to talk to a woman like that."

"Lydia's a whore. She was using me as much as I was using her."

"If you use someone, and it's mutual, you shouldn't have conversations like that."

Dick gritted his teeth. "I fucked her. I thought she was going to be my old lady. She put up with my asshole ways, and gave as good as she got. I don't know. I thought she was what I deserved for the shit I've done in this life."

"What changed?"

"I realized I couldn't stand her. I can't be with someone that I can't fucking stand. Her voice grates on my last nerve." He hadn't wanted Martha to find out about Lydia this way.

"Is that why you came to seek me out? To get

away from her?"

"One of my brothers told me that I deserved better. He believed I was sticking with Lydia as a punishment."

"Were you?"

"I didn't think I was worthy of anything else. You're going to wake up one day, and be thankful that I didn't kiss you earlier," he said.

She tilted her head to the side. Color started to seep back into her cheeks, and he wanted to reach out and touch her. He refrained from it. Dick didn't know how much he could handle, watching her, and not possessing her.

"So you didn't kiss me because you don't think you're good enough to be kissed?"

"I'm not good enough for you. I was an addict."

"And you wear the battles you've been in with pride. You're not trying to hide who you are."

He let out a sigh, staring down at the steaks. They were large, meaty, and looked delicious. "How do you want your steak cooked?"

"I like mine medium. There's going to come a point when you're going to need to wake up. If you don't, it's going to be years from now, and everything is going to be too late. You deserve love, Dick. You shouldn't settle for a woman just because she puts up with you."

"Becky put you through hell."

She laughed, and even the laugh had his pulse racing. "Dick, I don't think you're going to whore yourself out to the men around us. You're not like her. Never put yourself in the same league as her. You're two separate people. You're stronger than she ever was. Don't put yourself down. I'm so proud of you, and everything you've achieved."

He turned back to the grill, and put the plate down beside it.

"I wanted you to kiss me," she said.

Spinning back to face her, Dick was shocked to see she was telling him the truth. "What?"

"I wanted you to kiss me. I was disappointed when you didn't."

"You don't know what you're talking about."

"I do. You just don't understand what I want." She gave him a sad smile before leaving him alone.

Go and kiss her.

Go and show her how damn good it could be between the two of you.

He couldn't do either. Placing the steaks onto the grill, Dick kept cursing himself, and the phone call to Lydia.

Pulling his cell phone out of his pocket, he dialed Jessica.

She answered after the fourth ring.

"Why are you calling me?"

"Get Lydia out of my life."

"Sorry, buster, that's not something I can do. You do know I work, right? I'm at the hospital right now. You can't just order me around."

"I don't want her in my life."

"Then get your butt back to Piston County, and get rid of her."

"I've tried. She's not taking the hint."

He heard her sigh over the line. "Lydia will get the message soon. You've just got to be persistent."

Dick growled, at which Jessica chuckled.

"You're the one who screwed her, and brought her back into our lives. I'm done with her."

"You two were great friends."

"Exactly. We *were* great friends. We're not great

friends anymore. I can't stand her. I don't want to stand her, and she drives me fucking crazy."

He'd been trying to bring the two friends back together. Now he was seeing it was a waste of time. Jessica and Lydia's friendship was long gone. He'd been wasting his time all along.

"What do you suggest I do?"

"Ignore her. Don't call her. If she calls you, keep telling her the same old shit. The boys know you're done with her?"

"Yes, they know."

"Then give it time. Lydia will grow bored, and she'll move on."

"Thanks," he said.

They were both silent for a few seconds. Jessica was the one to break that silence. "Are you okay?"

"Yeah, why wouldn't I be?"

"I've not known you very long, Dick, but there's just something that seems up with you."

He released another sigh.

"See, that's what I'm talking about. You're sighing all the time."

"It's nothing." Was he sighing all the time? He wanted something that he couldn't have. Martha was driving him crazy, and he wanted to claim her as his own.

"I don't know what's going on with you, but take care."

"You're worried about me now?"

"You're part of Snake's world, and he's part of my world. Of course I care about you, and I care about him."

"It's nothing. I promise."

He turned the meat over and let it cook on the other side.

"So, where are you?"

"You're sticking around to have a conversation now?" he asked.

"What? It's my lunch break, and you interrupted me. The least you can do is talk to me."

"I've met someone." He cringed even as he said the words. He sounded like a fucking pussy, and he didn't want to sound like one. The brothers back home would be laughing at him if they saw him now.

"You've met someone."

"Well, I knew her when I was in rehab."

"She a hottie?"

"Yes."

I can't believe I'm talking to another woman about Martha.

I'm losing my mind.

There's no other word for it.

"Oh, how exciting."

"How is that exciting?" he asked.

"She knows about your drug taking past. She knows you're an asshole, and she hasn't kicked you in the balls. She must really like you."

Martha wanted me to kiss her.

She was disappointed that I didn't kiss her.

He was disappointed that he hadn't kissed Martha when he got the chance.

He didn't say anything else to Jessica.

"Oh, shit. We've had an emergency come in. Take care, Dick."

"Will do."

He hung up the phone, pleased the conversation had come to an abrupt end, and took the steaks off the grill. Martha had handed him two plates, and he pulled the clean plate out, and placed the steaks on top.

Making his way into the kitchen, he entered to

find Martha finishing off her salad.

"Is this all made with ingredients that you've grown?"

"Yes." She didn't turn to look at him.

Dick walked around behind her, placing the steaks to her right. He locked her into place by putting his hands either side of her, trapping her between him and the counter.

"What are you doing?" she asked.

"You wanted me to kiss you?"

"Go away. Go and enjoy the sun. I'll be done with this food in a moment. There's no point us both being stuck indoors."

He wasn't done with her. Pressing his body against her, he made her very aware of how aroused he was.

"What are you doing?" she asked, breathlessly.

"I didn't kiss you because you deserve someone a hell of a lot better than me."

Martha spun in his arms, and glared at him. "That's my choice to make, not yours."

"You're better than I am."

She kept shooting him a glare, and no matter what he did or said, she was fighting back. "No, I'm not better than you are. Don't you see the truth, Dick? We're both broken in our own ways. I can't go back to the life before Becky. Men know about her, and I can't just pretend that half of them didn't fuck her. I've seen some of the men who've shown an interest in me, and I've seen them going at my sister. She brought them here."

He cupped her cheek. "Stop."

"No. I'm not going to stop. I'm tired of being told how good I am, or what I should do. This is my life, and I should be the one to make the decision of what I want to happen in my life. Not you, not Becky, not anyone."

Tears were filling her eyes, and Dick hated it. Closing the distance between them, he slammed his lips down on hers. Sinking his fingers into her hair, he held her captive while he devoured her mouth. She tasted amazing, full, ripe, and perfect.

He'd never been much of a kisser before.

To him, kisses had been a waste of time when the main event of fucking was so much better. He liked fucking. Martha's lips were pure perfection.

Licking along her bottom lip, they moaned together, and Martha opened her lips, giving him access to her mouth. Sliding his tongue inside, he almost jumped back when she met him halfway, tasting him. Her hands slid up his chest, going around his neck.

With his other hand, he gripped her full hip, drawing her closer to him. This was the first real kiss he'd given a woman.

By the time he pulled away they were both panting. Martha's lips were red and swollen.

"The steaks are probably cold," she said.

He chuckled. "I can eat my steaks cold."

****

Later that night Martha touched her lips as she looked at her reflection in the mirror. She was twenty-eight years old and had been kissed by plenty of men. When she was younger, she'd made out with enough guys that she'd become adept at telling a good kisser from a bad one.

Dick knew how to kiss. He'd taken her completely by surprise with the way he trapped her against the counter, and now she didn't know how to think, or even how to feel. She was a ball of sensation. Her nipples were incredibly tight. Her arousal kept spiking, begging for Dick to come storming into her room, and have his wicked way with her.

Walking back into her bedroom, she was about to leave the room when her cell phone rang.

When she saw it was Lynne calling, she jumped onto the bed, and answered.

"What's up?" she asked.

"I was just making sure you were alive."

"Why wouldn't I be?"

"You never know. You've invited a stranger into your life. I was only making sure you've made it through the day."

"You're not very nice."

"I'm a very nice woman, Martha. I'm just a realist, and know the world is full of awful people who want to fuck you over."

Rolling her eyes, Martha sat up. "Why did you call?"

"I don't know. He seemed different to you."

"He is different." Running fingers through her hair, Martha tried to think of the right words. "He makes me feel alive, Lynne. I've never felt like this with a man, never."

"This isn't because of Becky, is it?"

Growling, Martha started to pace. "Not every part of my life is about her. She's my sister, and I loved her, but I've got to move on."

"I know you do, honey. I'm just worried about you. You've not got much in life."

I've got nothing.

"If this is a call to warn me, then please stop. I'm not going to do anything stupid. You've known me a long time. I like Dick. He's nice, and even though you don't get it, I do."

"I know. I know."

"I don't even know how long he's staying. I'm sure when he gets bored he'll move on, and I won't have anything to worry about."

"I'm really sorry."

Martha smiled. "Don't be sorry. Just try not to freak out and worry too much about me. I'd call you if I had anything to worry about."

"Okay."

After a couple more minutes of catching up, Martha hung up, leaving her phone by her bed. She walked downstairs to find Dick was already washed and sitting, watching the television.

"Hey," she said, walking into the room.

"Hey. What's wrong?"

"Nothing. I've had a call from Lynne. She wanted to make sure I was still alive." She gave a chuckle, making her way toward the sofa. Martha sat down, giving them enough distance. Her lips seemed to throb at the memory of what they'd shared in the kitchen. They hadn't talked about what happened between them. After the kiss, she'd finished preparing the salad. Then they'd gone outside, and she'd talked about her garden. They had shared a good dinner, and she loved the way he made her feel. It was natural between them, not false.

"She wanted to make sure I hadn't hurt you?" he asked.

"How do you know that?"

"I know friends like Lynne. It's good that she's worried."

Resting her head on the sofa, she stared back at him. "What about you?"

"What about me?"

"Has anyone called to tell you that they're worried?"

"Besides Lydia, I've done all the calling."

The mention of the women he'd been with chilled her arousal and wiped away any happiness out of her mind. He was with someone already. Why would he want her when he had another woman calling him up? "You've been with Lydia a long time?"

"No."

"If you can't stand her why did you even let her into your life?"

"You're all about the questions tonight, aren't you?"

"I'm sorry. You don't have to answer if you don't want to."

He reached across the sofa, and took her hand, locking their fingers together. "Lydia did something awful to her friend. I'm not going to get into it. I felt bad for her. I figured if I was with her, she'd make friends with the woman again."

"It didn't work that way?"

"No. It wasn't even close."

Martha licked her lips, wondering what to say.

"Stop doing that," he said.

"Stop doing what?"

"Licking those lips."

"Why?"

"You know why."

"I don't. I don't know what's wrong with licking my lips."

He moved a little closer to her, and Martha's pulse raced. His thumb glided across her bottom lip, and her pulse went into overdrive.

"You make me think about kissing you."

"I liked our kiss. I liked it a lot."

"You can have anyone you want."

"And yet, I want you."

He growled once again, and she couldn't help but smile. "You're playing with fire."

"Then burn me, Dick." For too long she'd been

playing the game of life being all safe, and always getting hurt. She no longer wanted to play it safe. Martha wanted to know what it was like to be desired, to be fueled by nothing but need.

Dick released her face, but before she had a chance to mourn the loss of his touch, he gripped her hips, and tugged her over his lap. She squealed, holding onto the back of the sofa as he placed her in position.

"At any time you want to stop, you tell me."

"I don't want to stop."

His hands moved from her hips gliding down to her ass.

"Do you have any idea what you're doing?"

"I've been wanting to do this from the first moment I met you." Sinking her fingers into his hair, she tugged the length back, making him lean back into her touch. Slamming his lips down on his, she moaned as she took possession of his mouth, kissing, and ravishing his mouth. Her pussy grew slick with need, and it was all need for him, consuming her.

"Fuck, baby, you're so fucking beautiful," he said, kissing down to her neck. One of his hands stayed on her ass while the other found its way into her hair, tugging her back.

Within seconds he had her on her back, and was staring down at her. He took over the kiss, commanding her with his presence, which surrounded her.

She was wearing a crop top, and he pushed the strap down off her shoulder, licking and sucking on her flesh.

"When I fuck you, you become mine," he said.

"Yes."

"You'll always be fucking mine."

Martha gasped as he pulled the shirt down, exposing her breast. She screamed out as he sucked her bud into his mouth. Pleasure exploded through every part of her being, and she held onto him tightly.

She tugged his shirt up over his body, and ran her hands all over him, loving the way he filled her hands. He was all hard muscle, a dangerous biker with his ink. She'd seen the one on his left shoulder, the skull and crossbones that seemed to her to relate more to pirates.

"Fuck, I wasn't going to do this," Dick said, suddenly pulling away.

Confused, Martha sat up.

Dick was wearing a pair of sweatpants, and his cock stood up, showing how much he'd enjoyed being between her thighs.

"What's the matter?"

"I didn't come here to fuck you, Martha. I wasn't looking for that."

"So? I wasn't looking for someone to have sex with. I want you. Our lives changed, and we were separated, and we've come back together."

"I'm not going to leave my club."

"I'm not asking you to leave anything. I'm not asking you to do anything." She ran fingers through her hair. "If you want to leave, you can leave. I'm not going to stop you. I've never begged a man to stay with me, and I'm not going to stop now."

She stood up, and feeling bold, she tugged her shirt off her body. Her pajama pants followed next until she stood before him completely naked.

"I want to fuck you, Dick. I'm not looking for forever, and I don't think you are either. You're here with me. You want me. Why don't we enjoy what we've got together?"

He shuffled forward on the sofa reaching out. She bit her lip as the tips of his fingers glided up the outside of her thighs. His gaze was on her pussy.

The tips of his fingers moved to the inside of her thighs, and he pressed them open. She opened her legs a little, keeping her hands at her sides.

His fingers didn't stop their teasing. He moved them up, caressing over her flesh until he was close to her pussy. She took several deep breaths, trying to control her need to pounce on him, and literally devour him.

When he was at her pussy, Martha moaned, and then cried out as he slipped his fingers through her pussy. She was soaking wet and probably should be embarrassed, but she wasn't. The last thing she felt was embarrassed. She was hot with a consuming need that was making it hard for her to think.

"You're lovely and wet."

"Do you like to talk throughout?"

"No. Usually I fuck until I come, and I don't give a fuck about the woman."

He looked up at her, and she kept his blue gaze. "Then what would you like?" she asked.

"I want you to lie on that coffee table, spread your legs open, and do exactly as I say."

Damn, she'd never been so turned on in her life.

The coffee table he was talking about was made of wood, and would take her weight.

Keeping her gaze on his, she lay down on the hard wood, which was long enough for her to be comfortable. She lifted her legs onto the ends of the table. He wasn't sitting directly in front of her but behind her.

"Open your legs wide," he said.

She spread her legs wide, opening them up for him to see.

Dick moved from the sofa, going to his knees at the edge of the coffee table. Suddenly, he moved, and placed a pillow beneath her head.

She stared down the length of her body, and watched as he once took a seat near her feet. His gaze wandered over her body, going over her breasts then down her stomach until he landed on her pussy.

"Do you like what you see?" she asked.

"Your pussy is glistening, and your cream is leaking down to your ass. You ever had a dick in your ass?"

"No."

Martha jumped as he ran his finger down one fold of her pussy lips. "I'm going to go and get a razor."

"What for?" she asked.

"I'm going to shave you, and then I'm going to lick this pussy until you're dripping into my mouth."

Before she had time to protest, he was gone.

Could she allow him to shave the most intimate part of her?

Crap, the feelings Dick was inspiring inside her were terrifying her. She'd not been lying when she told him that she didn't expect anything from him. Martha liked her lonely life where the only person she saw was Lynne. When Dick was ready to leave, she'd be able not to wait for him, couldn't she?

She really hoped so.

Chapter Six

Dick stopped in his room grabbing several condoms on his way back downstairs. He expected Martha to have moved, and was shocked to still find her laid on the coffee table.

"I'm not sure about you using a razor on me. It's very private down there."

"I'm not going to hurt you. I promise."

He placed a towel underneath her ass, and then went into the kitchen to fill a small bowl with water.

When he came back, she was still lying down, waiting. He loved her trust in him not to hurt her.

"I've not had anyone touch me down there, not with a razor."

"I'm honored I'm your first."

She chuckled. "You're going to be the first and the last."

"I'll make it good for you."

He started by soaping the fine hairs covering the lips of her pussy. Next, he started to trim away the excess of hair, catching it in the towel.

"I can't believe I'm lying like this, allowing you to do what you're doing," she said.

"It shows trust, baby."

When he'd finished with the scissors, he picked up the razor and set to work removing the fine hairs covering her pussy.

Every now and then he heard her catch her breath. He took his time, not wanting to rush it even though his dick was ready to explode from the pleasure.

When he was finished, he wiped the lips of her pussy, and went back to the kitchen to clean everything.

The moment he returned he saw Martha teasing her fingers through the bare lips of her pussy.

"It feels weird."

He moved toward the table and knelt back on the floor. Gripping her hips, he tugged her toward the edge of the coffee table. When she was in the position he wanted, he skimmed his fingers over her pussy. There was no trace of hair. He'd cleaned her up good and well.

"What are you thinking?" she asked.

Her cream was already leaking onto the lips of her pussy, and his mouth watered for a taste.

"I'll show you."

Without giving her a chance to tell him no, he gripped her hips, and flicked his tongue through her creamy clit. He circled her clit, moving down to fuck inside her pussy. Martha gripped the edge of the coffee table as he continued to lick, suck, and taste every part of her pussy. Without any hair, nothing got in his way, and he was able to taste her freely. He sucked one of her lips into his mouth, and Martha arched up into his touch.

"You don't have any idea what you're doing to me," he said.

"Please, I need to come."

"I'll let you come when I'm damn ready."

He teased the lips of her sex, sucking, and nibbling on the skin before sliding his tongue through her slit. When that wasn't enough, he fucked into her pussy. Her cream leaned down to the puckered hole of her ass, and he got his fingers nice and slick, and started to tease her anus.

At first she tensed up, but he didn't stop. He kept up his gentle touches without taking it too far, or making her uncomfortable. Dick wasn't in a rush. With his other hand, he slid one finger into her cunt, followed by a second. He pumped them inside her, relishing the feel of her pussy around his fingers. It wouldn't be long until he had her wrapped around his dick.

"I want you to come all over my finger."

She nodded, thrusting onto his fingers, and taking as much of him as she could. Martha was incredibly tight, and he knew he'd have to go easy on her the first time he fucked her.

"You're incredible, baby," he said, muttering the words against her skin, and biting down onto her clit. He sucked her clit into his mouth, flicking his tongue repeatedly over her nub.

"Fuck, that feels so good."

She screamed out, and her pussy started to clutch him in a desperation that took him by surprise. Within seconds she came, flooding his fingers with her juice. He didn't let up or stop teasing her pussy until she gripped his head tightly, practically yanking him away from his body.

He sat back, simply watching her come down from her high. Standing up after a few minutes had passed, he shoved the pajama pants down his hips, stepping out of them. He wrapped his fingers around his cock, working from the base up to the root. Dick wasn't circumcised, and there was no way any fucker was getting near to his dick with a knife or scissors.

Pumping the length, he stared down at her body. Martha sat up, turning her body so that she sat directly in front of his cock. She covered his fingers with her own, and moved in close. Her tongue peeked out, licking over the tip, tasting his pre-cum. Martha released a little moan before covering the whole head of his cock, and started to suck him inside her mouth.

Releasing his dick, he pulled her hair back, and simply admired the look of her lips wrapped around his dick. The sight turned him on, and it wasn't long before her hair was around his fist so that nothing got in the way of the view of her swallowing him down.

She bobbed her head onto his shaft, taking another inch deep into her mouth as minutes passed.

"Fuck, that feels so damn good," he said.

He started to work her mouth over his cock, making her take him deeper than ever before. She didn't gag, and she took him down, swallowing him.

Dick cursed, and it didn't take long before he was close to that point of no return.

"Martha, you've got to stop before I fill your mouth with my spunk."

She didn't stop, and hummed around his cock.

It was all too much. Gripping her hair tighter, he spilled his release into her mouth, and she swallowed him down, milking every last drop of his cum from his dick.

When there was nothing more, he pulled out, sinking down to his knees. "Where the fuck have you been?" he asked.

"I've been here for you."

He didn't care that her mouth tasted of his cum. Dick didn't care what had happened before her, or what evil shit had nearly destroyed them. He had to taste her.

Slamming his lips down on hers, he slid his tongue into her mouth, and waited for her to give in to him, to submit to his need to claim her.

Martha didn't put up much of a fight, and for that, he was so damn happy.

Dick picked her up, and they lay out on the sofa wrapped in each other's arms. He didn't want to let her go, not for a second.

"What else have you been doing with your life?" he asked.

"I've not done anything else. After I buried my parents, then Becky, I've stayed here, making a life for myself."

"Do you ever miss the outside world?"

She was silent for a second. He didn't rush her, waiting for her to talk to him when she was ready.

"Sometimes I miss it. I can get very lonely here all by myself. Most of the time, I don't. I listen to Lynne and what she has to say. What about you?"

"What do you want to know?"

"Do you love being part of a motorcycle club?"

"We sound like a bunch of pussies."

"Not at all."

He stroked her arm with the tips of his fingers. "I love the guys. They're my life."

"Did all of you go to rehab?"

"No. Some of us weren't addicted to the drugs or booze. Those who were, and wanted to remain in the club, went to rehab."

"Some of you didn't?"

"Five guys quit and left. We've not heard from them since."

"Isn't that dangerous?" she asked.

"No. They wouldn't rat on us. To be honest, I wouldn't be surprised to hear some of them were dead." He shrugged. Dick hadn't thought about the other guys who'd not wanted to deal with real life shit in so long.

"It must be hard for you all."

"No. We're a family, and we've got each other's backs." He nudged her forward, and walked to his room. Dick grabbed a small pouch that he kept for pictures. When he returned to the front room he saw Martha was about to put on her pajama pants. He tugged them out of her grip, throwing them across the room. Lying back on the sofa, he settled her between his legs. He wanted her naked. He liked having her wrapped around him with her naked flesh on his.

"What's that?" she asked.

"This is my family. It's the only family I've got." None of the club knew he had pictures of them all, or that he'd taken the time to get them developed. While he'd been packing with the intention of visiting Martha, he'd packed the pictures, hoping to share them with her. The first picture he pulled out made him smile. It was of Ashley and Mia, and just as quickly he was filled with pain.

"What is it?"

"That's Mia," he said, pointing to the dark haired woman. "She's with Curse. They're married. That," he pointed at the blonde, "is Ashley. She was a club whore, and she didn't want to be anything else."

"You sound sad. What happened to her?"

"How did you know anything happened to her?"

"You're in pain when you look at her. There's only one reason that will cause that, and it's because she's gone."

"She tried to help the club and ended up dead for her trouble. It hurt the club, almost killed Mia with the news, and Pussy, another brother who was close to Ashley. They were friends."

"This is sad, Dick."

"I know." He moved onto the next picture, which was of Mia and Curse. The next was of Lexie, Simon, and Devil. "He's the club president."

"President?"

"Yeah, he's the top guy at the club. He makes the decisions, and everything falls on him."

"I got it."

There were a couple of pictures of the kids playing in the clubhouse park.

"You've got a kids' park in the club?" she asked.

"Phoebe and Lexie demanded it." He pointed out Judi and Ripper, Death and Brianna. All of the club, and he even showed her the brothers who weren't taken.

"This is your family," she said.

"Yeah."

"They're really special, Dick."

"They are." He wanted to take Martha back to Piston County to meet his family.

****

Dick brought another picture forward, and it was of Devil with another man that she didn't recognize. They were standing with beers in their hands and looked around the same age.

"Who is that?" she asked.

"That's Tiny. He's the president of another MC, The Skulls. Things have been a bit tense with that club."

"How come?"

"Shit got said, shit went down, and we've got to fight for our club."

When he talked about The Skulls he grew tense.

"Are you okay?" she asked.

"Yeah."

"Do you like Tiny?"

"I like The Skulls. We all had a good thing going, and it was ruined for some pointless shit."

"I'm sorry you feel that way," she said.

He finished showing her some more of the pictures. Part of her was a little envious for the easy relationship he had with the people at the club.

She ran her hands up and down his thighs.

"I want to tell you that I'm clean," he said.

"What?"

"You sucked my cock. I wanted you to know that I was clean, and you didn't need to worry."

"I wasn't worried." She glanced behind her, and his gaze had already gone to her tits.

He placed the pictures on the floor beside the

97

sofa, and his hands skimmed up the side of her body, teasing up until his hands landed on her breasts. She stared at his hands as they slowly teased over her nipples.

Any thought of what they'd been talking about disappeared. She was always so sensitive when it came to her breasts. Biting her lip, she arched up, needing his rough touch. He wouldn't give it to her, and made sure his touch was light and gentle.

"You're wonderfully responsive to my touch, baby."

"Yes, I need you, Dick."

He moved down her body going between her thighs. "I'm not going to fuck you on the sofa. The first time I take you I want it to be on a bed."

Martha climbed off the sofa, and he took her hand. They made their way upstairs, but when he went to go to his room, she stopped him, tugging him into her own room. He didn't put up a fight.

Opening the door, she walked in, and Dick stopped her, tugging her close to him. He wrapped an arm around her waist, holding her close.

"I want to take you back to Piston County with me."

Martha froze. "Why?"

"I want you to meet my family, and to show you off."

She smiled. "Really?"

"Really. You're real, and I want to show the guys that you're real to me."

"We'll talk about it later."

He wrapped her hair around his fist, and tugged her close. In the next second he ravished her mouth, and any fear that had gripped her at him wanting to take her with him vanished. All she thought about was the way he touched her and held her close. His other hand ran up and down her body, gripping her ass then sliding down between her thighs. She opened her legs so he didn't have to fight in order to touch her.

"You're so fucking perfect, baby," he said.

She groaned out, thrusting her pelvis onto his hand, and enjoying the feel of his hands on her body.

He moved her back toward the bed, dropping her down onto the bed. Dick had already removed his hand from her hair, and she settled back away from the bed. "Fuck, I've forgotten the condoms."

She giggled as once again Dick left her.

With her facing the door, Dick would have a perfect view of what she was doing. Opening her thighs, she started to slide her fingers through her pussy, touching her bare flesh. It was weird to her to have a bare pussy, but the way he'd licked and sucked on her, she'd loved every second of it. Even when he moved on, she'd continue to remain bare.

Martha heard him coming up the stairs, and she settled down onto the bed, and teased her fingers through her pussy, growing more aroused with every passing second.

"Now that is the best sight in the world to see," he said.

She smiled, and kept on playing.

Finally opening her eyes, she saw him throw several packets of condoms onto the bed beside her head. There had to be at least five.

"I'm going to spend all night long playing with this body," he said.

"Are you sure you can go that long?"

"Are you kidding me? I'm being modest."

She chuckled. Dick batted her hand out of the way, replacing it with his own. She cried out, arching up into him as he plundered her pussy with two fingers.

Martha watched in amazement as he took the same fingers that had been inside her, and sucked onto them.

"You taste amazing."

He went again, teasing her clit, plunging a couple of fingers inside her, before removing them, and sucking the excess cream from the digits.

"You've no idea what you're doing to me," she said.

"You're soaking wet, and losing any sense of being ladylike."

"You don't want a lady in your bed?"

"No. I want a woman who knows what she wants. It's what I want, and you're going to give it to me."

She whimpered as he pressed a thumb to her clit, rubbing at the same time he pumped his fingers inside her pussy, driving her to the peak of pleasure.

When she was at the brink of orgasm, he pulled away, licking his fingers.

"Stop pulling away," she said, practically screaming the words at him.

In a quick movement, he flipped her onto her stomach, and slapped her ass three times.

Whack!

Whack!

Whack!

He didn't stop there, and he covered her back with his body, moving over here. Dick moved her hair out of the way, sucking on the flesh of her neck. She cried out at the instant contact, and she moaned, needing him to be closer.

"Don't ever try and lose your temper with me, baby."

"I can't believe you smacked my ass."

Dick moved off her long enough to place some pillows beneath her hips, raising up her ass. Next, he grabbed one of the condoms, tearing into the foil packet. She held her breath as the sound of his movements turned her on, and let her know he was putting the condom on.

One of his hands landed by her head, while his other guided his latex covered cock to her opening.

The moment the tip of his cock touched her entrance, Martha groaned. Just by the head of his cock on her pussy, she was aroused, and needing him deeper within her walls.

"Please, Dick."

"Are you going to be a good girl?" he asked.

"Yes."

"No more shouting out commands?"

"You're being a bastard."

He eased the tip within her, and she tried to take more of him but couldn't. Dick held her trapped so that he was the one in charge. He changed hands, and wrapped her hair around his fist, tugging her head back so that she looked at him. Dick kissed her lips, sliding his tongue into her mouth, making her melt on the spot. Tugging her hair to the left, he started to bite onto her neck, sucking on the flesh as he also used his teeth to drive her crazy. His cock remained so only the tip of him was inside her.

"No more shouting out commands? I'm the one in charge, not you?"

"Yes."

"You'll do as you're told?"

"Yes."

"Good girl." He slammed inside her, and Martha screamed out as he filled her. His cock was longer, thicker, and wider than any man she'd been with before. Even though it had been a good few years since she'd been with anyone, she'd have remembered a man like

Dick.

"Fuck!" He growled out the word, biting onto her throat and sucking the tender flesh. She knew exactly what he meant. It was fucking amazing. He paused deep inside her giving her the chance to get accustomed to the size of his cock. It was almost impossible to do with how deep he'd gone.

"One day I'm going to take you without the condom so I can feel how fucking wet you really are."

She loved his dirty talk. There was so much about Dick that she'd started to love. From the moment they first met she'd fallen in love with him. He pulled out of her so only the tip remained.

"Don't stop, please don't stop."

He didn't disappoint her, and thrust right back inside. Dick fucked her hard, to the point of pain, where the pleasure and pain mingled together. Her body was unused to having something inside her, and Dick was making her very much aware of how long it had been since she'd been fucked.

"I own you, baby. You're all fucking mine. I love this pussy. You're so fucking tight. I'm never going to want to leave."

Martha didn't want him to leave. She wanted him to stay, and to make love to her.

Shut up, Martha.

A few hours ago she'd promised him that she didn't want anything else from him.

It was lies, all of it.

Dick had invaded her heart years ago, and with him being close, he'd awakened a love she thought she'd never had. She'd been a complete and total fool.

Martha thrust up to meet each one of his, all the while her mind was being opened up, and there was no turning back.

She was in love with Dick, and it hadn't happened in the last day. It had happened all of those years ago.

****

Spider stood outside of Paris's house. It was in a good neighborhood, and he couldn't get his head around why she'd be working at a strip club. She clearly could have a life dancing professionally.

She wasn't working tonight, and instead of being at the club and supervising, he was back here, watching her house.

Finishing his cigarette, he stubbed it out, and made his way toward the front door. He couldn't get Paris out of his mind, and the more he thought about her, the harder it actually was to just get on with his life. Spider needed to know the truth.

Knocking on the door, he waited for her to answer.

Seconds later, Paris opened the door, and she was dressed like she would have been when she was leaving the club.

"What do you want?" she asked.

She crossed her arms over her chest, and he just couldn't help a glance at those full round tits. Paris had a nice set of tits when she got them out. Spider would be happy for her to keep them out on display all the time. He loved how she worked the crowd, only letting some men see them, and teasing others with what they could see. Some men didn't even realize that she hadn't shown them everything when she left stage. Paris gave them all a show, seducing all the men so that they were aroused to the point of pain when she got down to her underwear. Some of her moves on the stage imitated sex, making men think of being between her thighs, fucking her.

"I wanted to make sure you were okay."

"Is stalking in the contract at Naked Fantasies?"

"You know it's not." She was the only woman who'd sat down and read through the entire contract before signing it. "Can I come in?" he asked.

"You're not going to go away, are you?"

He shook his head. Spider needed answers.

"Fine."

She turned on her heel, and left the door open. Stepping through the door, he entered Paris's living space. It was like any other family home, complete with all the furniture, and pictures of a family.

Entering the living room, he stopped when he caught sight of Paris kneeling down beside a woman who looked a little younger than Paris, but this woman was playing with children's toys.

"Have you seen enough?" Paris asked.

"Okay, I'm just really confused."

Paris stroked the girl's hair, and nodded in Spider's direction. The woman looked exactly like Paris, and smiled at him. It was the way the girl was dressed that made Spider think she looked younger than Paris.

She moved toward his side, and urged him into the kitchen.

"Can she be left alone?"

"Yes."

"What the hell is going on? Why are you taking care of your sister?"

She bit her lip. "My parents died three years ago when I was eighteen. They were going to Fort Wills on a vacation where they first met, and there was a shootout. You might have heard of it, near a church. They had gone to visit the place where they were married, and they ended up dead."

Holy shit.

"The Skulls made sure that the families who were

living in Fort Wills were taken care of," Spider said.

"I'm not in Fort Wills. I live in Piston County, and at the time, I didn't get in touch with them. Asking for money, or anything, has never been my strong suit."

"So you're living here, struggling?" he asked.

"I promised my parents that if anything was to ever happen to them then I'd take care of Celia. I'm doing what I promised. Their insurance money only takes care of so much. The dancing, it helps."

"You've been taking care of her since you were eighteen?"

"Yes. She's my twin, my sister, and I love her. So that's my big secret. I'm not interested in forming connections to your club. I work for you, and it's easy, good money. I love to dance, I can't go to college, but at least I can dance for a living. It's not the best life, but it's my life, and it's the way I want to live it."

"You shouldn't be living like this. Chaos Bleed was there at the shooting. I'll talk to Devil, and we'll get this resolved."

"She is all the family I have. I don't want to get into any trouble."

Cupping her face, Spider stared down into her brown eyes. She was the most beautiful woman he'd ever met.

"Let me help you."

He had to help. The thought of her stripping again tore him apart inside. Paris needed his help, and he was going to help her.

Chapter Seven

Martha giggled as Dick took her down to the freshly mowed lawn and started to tickle her. He'd been with her about a week now, and it had been the best week of her life. With his help, she'd finished planting her vegetables, completed the weeding, and built a couple of wigwam style tubs for her beans to run up. She couldn't remember the last time she'd had a day of fun. Today, besides watering her plants, was a day of fun.

She'd offered to take Dick into town, but he'd wanted to stay at home, and she wasn't going to complain. During the day they worked, and Dick even did a few odd jobs around the house for her. The edge of the roof was no longer crumbling down. He'd fixed everything, and she no longer had a plumbing problem.

By night, she belonged to Dick, and he spent many hours making her addicted to his touch. Her own addiction wasn't even spent with the way he touched her. Lynne talked to her every day to make sure she was alive, but that question had taken a back seat. Dick had proven to Lynne he wasn't going to kill her.

"Stop, stop, stop," she said, giggling. They were sprawled out on the lawn, and he settled between her thighs. The hard length of his cock pressed against her front, making her aware that he was aroused.

She moaned, arching up against him.

Their play took a sudden turn, and Dick's fingers were teasing her, working the strap of her shirt down her arm.

"We're all alone out here," he said.

"We are." She wasn't going to argue with him. They were alone together. Martha lived a secluded life, a solitary one, and she'd not been lying when she said she did.

Down the strap went followed by the strap of her bra. She bit her lip as he exposed her breast. "I love your tits. I love how big they are."

"They're not too big?"

"No, they're fucking perfect. I want you all the time, Martha."

He'd been talking to his brothers back at Piston County. She knew he missed his family.

"I want you, too."

"This isn't something I can walk away from," he said, surprising her.

"I don't know what to make of that." She rested her head on her hands, and smiled up at him.

"You know what I mean by that. You're just being a little difficult."

"When we talked last time, you didn't want to make this complicated. I don't want to make this complicated either."

"Then let's not make this complicated. It's just us, but I want you to know I want more."

She touched his pulse at the base of his neck, which was beating rapidly. "I can't leave here. I like it here."

"What if I can give you this, at my place?"

Martha didn't know how to answer him. She was afraid, scared to believe it was possible.

"You'd want this kind of life."

"I'd live here with you if I was given the chance. I'm part of Chaos Bleeds, and I know if we're close to my brothers, they'd protect you."

"I don't need protecting." She thought about Becky and the way she'd looked on the last day that she saw her. It had been awful, disgusting, and one image that Martha couldn't get out of her mind.

"Everyone needs protecting."

Dropping her hand from his pulse, she bit her lip. "Maybe I should come and visit you? Would that help?"

"I'd like to take you with me back to Piston County."

She glanced around at her garden. She'd be able to leave it for a week or so, nothing more.

"When would you like to go back?" she asked.

"Not yet. I want to stay here with you, in this little world. In fact, I was thinking it's a Friday, and I've spoken to Lynne, and she's in agreement. It's time for us to go out, and to go dancing."

"You want to go dancing."

He scrunched up his face. "Not really but I've been talking with your friend, and she told me how much you love dancing."

"You'd go dancing for me?"

"Yes, I'd go dancing for you."

"It's not that bad, surely."

"No, it's not that bad, but we're talking about dancing."

She laughed. There was no way to control her smile.

"I know and if dancing with you puts that kind of smile on your face, then I want to do it. I want to dance with you."

Martha cupped his cheek once again, running her thumb over his bottom lip. "I've really missed you."

She wasn't comfortable telling him that she loved him, not yet. Dick was unlike anyone she'd ever met, and she didn't want to change him, not one bit. He'd been to hell and back, and lived to tell the tale. She didn't see his past fight with addiction as something to be repulsed by, but something to cherish. He'd come back from whatever dark place he'd been at, and she was so happy he'd come back to her.

Dick pulled the strap of her shirt back down, and she didn't fight him. Arousal flooded her once again, and she moaned as the light breeze danced across her nipple. She was already turned on, and the breeze made her nipple pucker even harder.

"So beautiful," he said.

She loved the way he was always complimenting her. Martha wasn't used to being complimented. She was used to being overlooked.

Pushing all those doubts aside, she relished the feel of him close to her. He kissed her neck going down to her nipple. She stared down as he circled her nipple with his tongue then bit down with his teeth. Martha cried out, arching up against him.

With his other hand, he slid it up her thigh. She wore a pair of loose shorts, and it didn't keep him out. He went underneath her shorts, cupping her naked pussy. Martha loved having a bare pussy, so she hadn't even allowed any pubic hair to grow back.

She wasn't wearing any panties so the moment he touched her pussy, his fingers stroked over bare flesh.

"You're already wet for me."

He pushed two fingers inside her pussy, at the same time he sucked her nipple deep into his mouth.

The double hit of pleasure was just too much. She wriggled underneath him, trying to get closer, but needing him to make it a little harder.

She tugged at his shirt, tearing it away from his body.

They wrestled on the ground, and Martha pushed him back until he was underneath her, and she was straddling his waist.

"Now that's better," she said.

"I'm the one in charge," he said.

She shook her head. "You've been in charge at

night. This is my lawn, and I'm on top. I'm going to play a little."

Martha pulled her shirt and bra off, loving the freedom of being naked, and outside in the fresh air. He didn't fight her. All it would have taken from him was a quick push, and he'd have been on top.

Dick was naked beneath her, and she ran her fingers over his chest, sliding her fingers over his nipples.

She traced her fingers over some of his ink, the name "Chaos Bleeds" was inked across his heart.

"I love your ink," she said.

"It means something to me."

"The club means something to you."

"Chaos Bleeds was my salvation."

"You really believe you're unlovable, don't you?" She tilted her head to the side while she observed him.

"I'm the man that I am."

"And you don't think that man deserves to be loved?" she asked.

"I've done a lot of bad shit, Martha. I've killed people."

"Were they innocent?" She didn't for a second believe Dick was a bad person. He was a person who'd been hit by a hard life, and there was no sign of it ever going away. She would take it away from him, if he let her. Martha knew all about pain, and how hard it was to carry on with a life that seemed destined to shit on you.

"No."

"Then I don't need to hear anymore. We do what we need to in order to survive. You've survived, and you shouldn't try to fight it, baby. You've done your fighting." She stroked her fingers over the past wounds of his addiction. "You've come out the other side stronger than ever."

She leaned down, kissing his lips, then following a path down his each of his arms. When she'd gotten her point across, she stood over him, and worked her shorts down her legs.

He did some odd shuffling movement, kicking off his jeans. She straddled his waist once again, reaching behind her to grip the hard length of his shaft. Working from the base up to the root, she started to masturbate him, getting him harder still.

Not once in all of the years she'd lived in this house had she ever had the guts to fuck outside.

Dick grabbed a condom out of his jeans, and handed it to her. "If you want to be in charge, you get to wrap him up."

She giggled, taking the condom from him. "It would be my pleasure."

Tearing into the condom, she worked down his body, cupping his cock. With Dick's gaze on her, she wrapped her lips around the tip, and swallowed him down.

"Fucking shit, so fucking good."

Cupping his balls, she worked them between her fingers at the same time she sucked on his cock, lathering the tip, tasting his pre-cum, then taking more of him into her mouth.

She moaned around his shaft, trying to take more of him. When she got to the point that she might have gagged, she moved off him.

"I don't want to come in your mouth. If you keep that up then I'm going to have no choice but to. I want inside your pussy."

Leaving his cock, she pressed a final kiss to the tip then rolled the condom over his cock.

Martha straddled his waist, and lowered herself

over his cock, crying out as she slammed down onto his length, and he went so damn deep. A week of fucking him, and she still hadn't grown accustomed to the depth of him, or the width.

"Fuck, baby, that is so fucking good."

She agreed with him. It was so fucking good, amazing even.

"That's it, baby, work my dick. It belongs to you, only you."

"Yes, Dick, please."

Bouncing on his cock, she took him all the way inside. Dick went from touching her breasts, to stroking between her thighs.

"My cock splits the lips of your pussy open, and I can see everything, baby. You're taking my dick so damn beautifully. Fucking amazing, it's the perfect sight."

She glanced down, and watched as he opened her pussy lips a little more. Martha started to tease her pussy, stroking her clit over and over again.

"Yes, yes, yes," she said, shouting the words repeatedly.

Dick gripped her hips, thrusting up inside her. Martha's orgasm washed over her, and she ground her pelvis onto his.

With three quick slams up inside her, Dick came, roaring out his pleasure.

When it was over, she collapsed over him, panting for breath. The sun beat down on them, and Martha was content.

"That was fucking amazing," he said.

"I know."

He ran his hands over her back, caressing her. She closed her eyes, and it wasn't for the first time in her life, Martha was terrified of losing someone she loved.

****

"You love her, don't you?" Lynne asked later that night.

Dick looked toward her friend, who was standing in the kitchen, sipping a cool sweet tea. "Why do you want to know?"

"She's my friend. I care about her, and she's different."

"What do you mean?"

Lynne released a sigh, but she kept her gaze on him at all times. "I've not seen Martha so happy before."

"What do you mean?"

"I've grown up with her, and with Becky. They were like two opposites, and it was so fucking crazy at times. I always wanted to be a lawyer, and Martha always wanted what her parents had, which was this." Lynne glanced around the room. "Growing up, Martha would have boyfriends, and Becky would take them from her. Whatever Martha wanted, Becky wanted. Their parents saw through Becky's selfishness, and so Martha was never overlooked. She always got rewarded for her grades, and what she achieved. Becky was scolded when she was in trouble. They were a good family."

"Why do I get the feeling that I'm going to wish that I had smothered the fucking bitch while I was in rehab?"

"As a lawyer, I'm going to pretend that I didn't hear that."

"You can pretend all you want. I didn't kill Becky. I can make idle threats." He folded his arms over his chest, waiting for her to speak.

"Anyway, Becky went out of her way to make life hell for Martha. She stole her boyfriends, stole some of Martha's homework. All the time, Becky did this, Martha wouldn't say anything. It would drive me crazy. The teachers knew what was going on, and would report

Becky."

"Martha never allowed herself to get close to anyone, no guy, nothing because she figured it would be taken off her in some way?" Dick asked, already getting the gist of what Lynne was trying to tell him.

"Yes."

"I'm not going to leave her."

"You love her?"

"Yes, I do. I've loved her since I've been in rehab."

"Then where were you?" Lynne asked.

"I didn't even know I loved her, Lynne. I'm not the perfect guy, okay? I've not understood what I've felt, but I do now."

"Please, I'm begging you, Dick, don't break her heart."

Lynne's eyes were filled with tears as she said those words.

"I'm not going to."

"I know you're not going to on purpose. I imagine all of those boyfriends didn't mean to break her heart, but they all did. She wouldn't tell me how much it hurt, and she'd lie to me now." Lynne pushed out a breath. "All I ask is that you don't break her heart."

"I'm not going to break her heart. I have no intention of hurting her." He was going to protect her, love her for the rest of his life, and that thought alone terrified him. Martha deserved a man with a good past, a kind heart, and someone who hadn't fought with addiction. Yet the thought of another man touching her filled him with so much anger.

"Hey," Martha said, walking into the kitchen.

Lynne turned away, finishing her drink. From the look on Martha's face, she didn't have a clue what they'd been talking about. She wore a simple yellow summer dress with spaghetti straps. Her hair was pulled up on top of her head with little curls cascading around her face. She looked so beautiful.

He was the luckiest man in the world as far as he was concerned. "What's the matter?" Martha asked.

"Nothing. Lynne's just checking to see if her date was going to meet us here or at the bar."

Lynne pulled out her cell phone, sending a quick text.

"I half expected to come down here and to find you both tearing each other apart."

"I come in peace," Lynne said. "He makes you happy, and so he's protected from my wrath. It's when he hurts you that he needs to back the fuck down."

Martha chuckled.

The cell phone pinging echoed in the room.

"William is meeting us at the bar," Lynne said. "He's already there."

"Are you riding with us?" Martha asked.

"Nah, I'm going to take my car in case William turns out to be a bit of a dud. You know I've not got the best sense when it comes to men," Lynne said.

They locked up the house, and Dick made his way toward Martha's car. He'd already taken a long look under the hood, and made any repairs that she'd needed. In the week that he'd been away from Chaos Bleeds he'd found himself once again. He was no longer controlled by his addictions, and he'd rediscovered his love for machinery. Dick had ordered the parts for Martha's car, then changed them with her watching him. He'd not done any work on a car in over six years. Chaos Bleeds owned a mechanic shop as they were all picky about who worked on their bikes. This was the first time he'd worked on a car that wasn't his own.

Climbing behind the wheel, he turned over the

ignition, and the car purred to life.

Martha let out a little whoop. "My car hasn't done that in years."

"I've fixed it, and your baby is as good as new."

"I didn't know you were a mechanic."

"I am. I've just not used any of my skills in years."

Lynne pulled out of the long drive first, and Dick followed behind her. He wanted tonight to be fun for Martha, a chance for her to forget everything else, and just enjoy life.

They made their way toward the bar in town where he'd first met Martha a little over a week ago. He parked up, and made Martha sit until he helped her out of the car.

"You're a real gentleman," she said.

"Keep that little detail to yourself. You'll ruin my reputation."

She chuckled, and Lynne walked toward them. Dick took Martha's hand, and they all walked toward the bar.

Lynne took them to a table near the window where a guy Dick had never seen before was waiting.

"Martha, I'd like you meet William. He's a defense lawyer at the firm that I work for," Lynne said.

After all the introductions were made, he went to the bar, and ordered them some drinks. William came with him.

"Lynne told me you were a biker," William said.

"And?" He pulled some cash out of his back pocket, and stared at William.

"Just saying, if you need any help in the future let me know."

"We've got our own lawyer who can handle our problems. You don't need to start worrying about us." He paid for their drinks, not giving William the chance to pay. They walked back to the women, and Dick slid into the booth.

He made small talk, listening as Martha questioned William. At first he tensed up, wondering if she was interested in the guy, but then he realized she was looking out for her friend. After their first drink, he took Martha's hand, and led her onto the dance-floor. The bar was getting busy, and it gave him an excuse to pull her in close to his body.

"Are you having fun?" he asked.

"The best fun."

"Good. I want you to be happy."

"You make me happy, Dick. Always."

He pulled her in close, and started dancing with her. The bar became really crowded, but Dick didn't care so long as he had his woman in his arms. That's what Martha was. She was his woman.

The woman he loved with all of his soul.

"You make me happy as well, baby, more than you will ever know." She was his other half, and his very reason for living.

She rested her head on his chest, and he held her even tighter. When the song changed, they went back to their table at the same time as Lynne and William. They ate some food, and went back to the dance-floor. It had been years since Dick had enjoyed going on a date, and taking time away. Martha was the reason he was having such a good time. He loved her, and she'd broken through his hard shell, to find the man within. Before going into rehab he'd been nothing, simply existing. The moment he talked to her, he'd wanted to be better for her.

It was getting late when shit started to get serious. A crowd of rowdy men had walked into the bar, and the atmosphere seemed to change. The moment Martha and

Lynne caught sight of the men, they seemed to freeze. Their happiness died in that moment.

"Is everything okay?" Dick asked.

"Yeah, it's fine," Martha said.

"Well, isn't it little Martha." The man at the head of the group spoke up, making his way toward the table. "It has been too long since you've been here. I was wondering what happened to all the free pussy."

Dick got out of his seat, and William did the same. It would seem the lawyer didn't like Martha being insulted.

"You need to leave," Dick said.

"Fuck off, man. Martha's just like her sister, ready to spread her legs for a little bit of blow. First she's got to do me before she gets anything else."

Martha climbed out of the booth. "Forget about it. Let's go."

"What's the matter, baby? Don't you want your new boyfriend to know that you spread them like your sister? They test your sister, then you. Two fucking sisters. Shame Becky's dead, she always knew how to give good head."

Dick had heard enough. Stepping up close, he got right into the man's face. "Back the fuck down before I break your fucking face," he said. He wasn't afraid.

"Fuck off, Charles. You don't need to be here," Lynne said.

"Whoa, you boys are going for a gangbang—"

He'd heard enough. Slamming his fist into Charles's face, he finally brought a stop to the vulgar language. The last thing he wanted was for Martha to be listening to the bastard's vile insults.

William started in on the other guys, but Dick was only interested in the fucker who was near him. He started to beat the shit out of him.

It didn't take long until an all-out fight broke out. Dick made sure by the time he left the bar that Charles knew not to even start on Martha again.

Before the cops arrived, he and William rushed out to the waiting women. Lynne was in her car, and she gave him a thumbs-up. Martha was already seated behind the wheel. Climbing into the passenger side, he closed the door at the same time she took off.

"Are you completely insane?"

"Is that the kind of shit you've had to put up with?" he asked, giving her a question instead of answering one.

"It doesn't matter what I have to put up with. I can't believe you just did what you did."

"I protected you, okay," he said.

"That wasn't protection."

"Tell me now, right to my face, that the fucker I've just hit hasn't been tormenting you for months? Tell me?"

She went silent.

"He's lucky I've walked away with him fucking breathing."

"We could have just left. It didn't have to be difficult."

Dick shook his head. "You shouldn't have to run away. You shouldn't have to run from fuckers like that." He slammed his fist against the dashboard. "Has he always been like that?"

"He was one of Becky's boyfriends. I never dated him, but he's the one that started the rumors." She shrugged.

He couldn't believe it, and the sight of her just shrugging her shoulders pissed him off.

"You could get into trouble."

"The way he was talking, he'd keep his mouth

shut."

"Why?"

"He was talking about drugs. Blow, that's a fucking drug. If he knows what's good for him, he'd just say it was a fight between friends that got out of hand." Dick knew men like that. He used to have to deal with assholes like that to get his gear. Fuck, it was a whole other life.

Martha was shaken, and now he needed to repair that damage.

Chapter Eight

Slamming the car door closed, Martha didn't even wait for Dick to enter her home. She left the front door open but stormed right upstairs to the bedroom. Pacing the room, she heard him stand in the doorway.

She glanced toward him, and he was leaning against the doorframe, looking way too relaxed.

"Why?"

"He spoke to you like shit."

"So?" She was confused.

"You're my woman, Martha. You belong to me."

"You don't even know me."

"I fucking know you. You're not the kind of woman who allows a man to fuck her, and let other men treat her like that. You belong to me, and I take care of what is mine."

She just stopped, staring at him. "This is nonsense. You're not making any sense."

"No, I'm making sense. You're just not used to having people care about you."

"I know what it's like to have people care about me."

"Do you?" he asked. "Or are you used to caring about everyone else? Everyone you've ever loved has left you at some point. I'm not leaving you."

"You're here for vacation. You're going to be gone, and then what happens?"

He laughed, which just set her temper aflame. Grabbing the nearest thing to her, which happened to be a book, she threw it at him. She was the worst shot ever, and the book landed on the doorframe, nowhere near him.

"It's okay for you. You've got a whole MC back home. You have a family who care. I've got no one. That little fight could cause me so much pain."

He shook his head and entered the room.

She took a step back, but he didn't stop in his advance. He stood directly in front of her. Martha wasn't afraid even as he cupped her face, and held her in place.

"You don't get what I'm saying to you, baby. You belong to me. I love you. I've loved you from the moment I first saw you in the rehab center, and I love you now. You're not getting rid of me."

His admission left her literally speechless. What the hell was she supposed to say to that?

"You love me?"

"Yes, I love you."

Wrapping her arms around his neck, she held onto him tightly. "I love you, too." She'd been so afraid to voice her own thoughts that she'd kept it all locked in tight.

"I'm not letting you go. I'm many things, baby, but I can't let any bastard speak to you that way. You're mine, and I take care of what is mine."

Tears filled her eyes, and before she could stop them, they started to fall away.

"I can't believe you love me. It seems almost too good to be true."

"I know. I'm an amazing person."

"What are we going to do?" she asked.

"What about?"

"You live in Piston County. I live here. That's not going to be easy to fix."

"We're not going to try to fix it, baby. We're going to make it work," he said.

He started to caress her back, and Martha's body awakened with need. It took her by surprise, and yet it didn't. This was what Dick did to her: he woke her up, mending her broken heart.

Dick worked the zipper at the back of her dress, and pulled it down. She whimpered as the tips of his fingers grazed her back. It felt so damn good, and yet it wasn't enough.

He removed the dress from her body, and she stepped out of it. Reaching behind her back, she unhooked her bra. As she removed her underwear from her body, Dick started to tug off his own clothing.

When they were both naked there was no separating them. She jumped into his arms, wrapping hers around his neck. Slamming his lips down on hers, Dick picked her up, and dropped her onto the bed, following her down. He settled between her thighs, and his dick worked between the lips of her pussy.

Dick started to slide his cock up and down, going over her clit with each stroke of his cock.

"Lie back."

She shuffled up the bed as he made his way down her body, kissing every inch of her. He licked her breasts, circling the buds before moving down. Dick rested his hand on her stomach, keeping her in place as he worked her pussy. He opened the lips of her pussy, opening her up for his mouth, and he sucked her clit into his mouth.

Moaning, she arched up against him, needing the pleasure that only he could give.

Dick flicked his tongue over her clit then moved down to slide within her pussy. He fucked her with his tongue, making her yearn for his cock.

She was shaking, and Dick refused to let her reach orgasm. He'd fuck her pussy then glide up to suck her clit into his mouth. The torture went on and on.

"Please, Dick, I can't take much more. I need you, please."

Over and over, she begged him.

He wouldn't listen, keeping her at the peak but

not letting her go over the edge. She didn't think she could handle whatever he was doing to her. Pressing a hand to her stomach, he kept her in place as he bit down on her clit.

"Come for me."

Martha screamed out, sinking her nails into the flesh of his arms. She couldn't keep the sounds to herself, and she gave it her all.

While she was still coming down from her orgasm, Dick grabbed a condom, sliding it over his cock.

In the next second, he was inside her, trapping her arms above her head so that he was the one in control.

"I love you," he said.

She smiled. "I love you, too."

He pulled out of her pussy so that only the tip remained and then slammed the whole length inside her. "No other man is going to know how damn good this pussy is. I'm going to get my name inked on you so everyone knows who you belong to."

"I'm going to have Teddy Bear inked on my skin."

Dick silenced her with a kiss, fucking her so that her headboard hit the wall with the force of his thrusts.

The rest of the night, Dick made love to her, making her forget about the trouble that occurred at the end of the night.

****

Dick stared down at Martha the following morning. She was fast asleep, and he didn't blame her. He'd kept her up until four fucking her, making love to her. She must have experienced over five orgasms last night at his hands.

He'd done it to make her forget about what he'd done. Dick didn't regret beating the shit out of Charles. The bastard had it coming to him after what he said to

Martha. He didn't agree with any fucker saying vile shit to a woman, let alone Martha.

It was a little after six, and he'd only had a couple of hours sleep, yet he couldn't bring himself to sleep any longer.

Pulling on a pair of jeans, he left Martha to sleep, and made his way down to the kitchen. He placed the coffee machine on before going outside. It was still early enough that he grabbed the hose pipe, turned the tap on, and started to water all of the fruit and vegetables. He liked watering plants. The simple action calmed him.

Pulling out his cell phone he dialed Devil's number. He wasn't surprised when Devil answered after a couple of rings.

"What's the matter?" Devil asked.

"Nothing. I was just calling in."

"At six in the morning?"

"It's been a busy night."

"What did you do?" Devil asked.

"I got into a fight. It was no big deal. An asshole was trying to measure his dick by the shit awful statements he said to my woman. I told him how it was going to be, only I used my fucking fists. Is Simon back in school?"

"Yes, he's learning, and his teachers have said it is like a miracle transformation. I almost told them it was all about the pussy." Devil snorted. "Fuck me, I could have Tabitha as my daughter–in-law. I'm getting too damn old."

Dick snorted, and saw that Martha had entered the kitchen. She wasn't much of a sleeper either.

"I called because I want to bring Martha home with me."

"This the woman you're staying with?"

"Yes. I want her to come and meet the club, and

the guys."

"You know Lydia's hanging around still?"

"I know. I've told her more than once that we're over. She doesn't seem to be taking the hint."

"This is the hint you're going to be giving her?"

"This isn't about me. I want Martha to stay with me. Speaking of, you know that house three down from where you live? It has the small front yard, but large back that has different sections, perfect for growing?" Dick asked.

"What about it?"

"Is it still available?"

"Yeah."

"I want it."

"This with Martha is serious?"

"It's more serious than anything." He watched as Martha opened the door and grabbed two cups. She wore one of his shirts and nothing else. Her hair was knotted on top of her head, and she looked beautiful. The sight of her made him want to take her to bed. "I'm in love with her, Devil. I want her as my old lady. I need her in my life."

"Fuck me, you've finally fallen in love."

"Yes."

"All right. Congratulations."

"Thank you."

"When will you be coming home?"

"In a couple of days."

Martha walked over to him, holding the two cups. He finished his call with Devil and put his cell phone away.

"Important call?" she asked.

"That was Devil. He's Prez of the MC. I'm just letting him know that we're coming home."

"Are you sure it's a good idea taking me with

you?" she asked.

"It is."

She nodded.

He took the coffee from her, sipping at the dark liquid.

"Are you still mad at me?"

"About last night?" she asked.

"Yes."

"No, I'm not mad. I got used to the name calling and all the other crap, and I shouldn't have." She took a sip of her coffee. "I can't believe I let it get that bad."

"Did you always walk away?"

"Yes. I'm not much of a person for fighting. I didn't even stand and fight with the bank guy. I complained to his boss."

"You shouldn't have to fight assholes like that."

"I can't believe you beat him up."

He shrugged. "The bastard went too far."

"You weren't scared? You were outnumbered."

"No, I wasn't scared, and I didn't give a shit if I was outnumbered. No one bullies a woman like that, not where I come from."

She took another sip of her coffee and smiled at him over the rim of her cup. "You know, for a guy who is supposed to be an asshole, you're not doing a very good job of actually being one."

"I'm an asshole where it counts."

Martha chuckled. "I'm going to go and get dressed."

"You don't have to get dressed on my account."

"I do. We've got Lynne and William coming around for breakfast. She texted me last night, and I've only just seen my phone. I'm not going to run around naked with my friends here."

"You're coming with me to Piston County on

Monday?" he asked.

She turned around to smile at him. "I wouldn't miss it."

He watched her cute ass walking away from him. She really had mended his broken heart. Until she'd appeared in his life, he'd been broken inside. She was making him whole, and he was sure she didn't even realize what she was doing.

****

"What's going on?" Lexie asked, walking into the kitchen to find Devil looking down at his phone. It was Saturday so the kids weren't at school. From the sounds coming from the living room they were already awake. Devil always allowed her to sleep in on Saturdays. It was the only day where she got the chance to relax.

"It was Dick."

"What about him?" she asked, going to the fridge for some juice.

She couldn't have caffeine as she was breastfeeding their son.

"I've got to call the realtor. He wants that house three doors down."

She frowned, turning to look at her husband. There was a twenty year age gap between them, but to Lexie, age was just a number. She loved Devil, and knew he would never allow anything to happen to her. Their love had been scary as hell, but something she wasn't ever going to regret. They were a family, and the Chaos Bleeds crew was part of her life as well.

"This is Dick we're talking about?"

"Yes."

"Wow, he's met someone?"

"Yes."

She poured some juice into a glass and took a sip. "I guess I'll get on the phone to Tracy. She's the one who is dealing with that house. Will we get to meet the woman?"

"Yes. Dick's bringing her home."

"What about Lydia?"

"I guess he's hoping to get rid of one using the other." He shrugged.

Walking behind him, she started to rub at his shoulders. "What's the matter, baby?"

"Nothing, life is moving so damn fast, and I worry that it's time to hand over the gavel."

"Like Tiny has?"

"Yeah." He leaned back against her, and she pressed a kiss to his forehead.

"You're not like Tiny or The Skulls. None of the guys will ever allow you to step aside, not right now."

He sat forward running a hand down his face. Lexie hated it when he was like this. Devil at times had the weight of the world on his shoulders, and it didn't need to be like that.

"This shit with Master. I don't know what to fucking do."

"Be alert and wait. There's nothing else you can do."

She wished there was something else she could say to make him see reason. Devil rarely doubted himself, and yet that was exactly what he was doing.

"I can't let anything happen to you and my family, Lex. I wouldn't forgive myself."

"Nothing is going to happen. Stop the worry talk, and just relax. We've all got to learn to take what life throws at us." She kissed his cheek. "Now, make your pancakes."

He chuckled, gripping the back of her neck, and ravishing her mouth. "Say please."

Chapter Nine

"You're going to Piston County?" Lynne asked.

William and Dick were outside talking and watering the plants again. They had stayed throughout the day, and now she and Lynne were making dinner for them.

"Yes."

"What was that last night? He went a little crazy don't you think?"

"He didn't like the way Charles was talking to me. He doesn't think it's right that I'm the one running away." She shrugged. "It makes sense."

"I've not got a problem with what he did last night. It was about time someone put Charles in his place. Dick cares about you, Martha."

"I know." She tucked some hair behind her ear and smiled at her friend. "He told me he loved me."

"No shit?"

"Yes. He told me last night. We're going to Piston County because he wants me to meet his club, and I really want to go. Will you please keep an eye on my home while I'm gone?"

"Keep an eye?"

"You know, water everything, and just show it a bit of love."

"I'm not a gardener."

"You don't have to garden, just stand with the hose pipe for an hour, if that, to make sure the plants get plenty of water. I can pay you."

"Don't even think about offering me money. That's insulting, and I don't like it." Lynne crossed her arms over her chest, and nodded. "Fine. I'll take care of your plants. You've got to tell me everything about Piston County, and the biker club."

"I will. I promise."

"Martha?" Lynne asked.

"Yes."

"Do you love him?"

"I do. I love him so much, and it scares me." She paused in cutting the onion. "Everyone I love has been hurt. It scares me to let him know how much I love him."

"What happened with Becky, it wasn't your fault."

"I know that. I do. It's just hard not to think that the world is out to get you. It feels like it." She wiped at her eyes with the back of her hand. "I don't want to get into it now. I'm sorry. I shouldn't have brought it up."

"Don't, Martha. I mean it."

"You don't even like Dick."

"After last night, I'm his number one fan. He's the first guy that I've seen who was prepared to stand up for you. I have a lot of respect for him. You need a guy like that in your life." Lynne wrapped her arms around her. "I'm going to miss you."

"I'm not leaving for good."

"I know. I'm just so happy that you're happy. It seems too damn long since you were happy." Lynne kissed her head before pulling away.

"What about William?" Martha asked. "How is that going?"

She quickly directed the questions at her friend's love life rather than her own. They cooked together, laughing and talking to each other. Martha loved being with Lynne, and she loved looking out of the window to see Dick walking around the garden. This was her life, and to her it couldn't get any better. It was perfect.

Later that night after Lynne and William had gone, she leaned back against Dick as they both stared up at the stars. It was late, but it was still warm outside.

"I love being here," he said.

"I do, too."

"I want to share my life with you, Martha."

"Do you think we're moving too fast?"

"Do you?"

She took a minute to think about it. "No."

"I don't either. Life is too damn short, and it's easily gone. One moment we're alive, kicking, and the next we're dead." He locked their fingers together, and she stared down at where they were connected.

"I'm pleased you didn't die like Becky did."

"I'm not going to die like she did either. I'm not going to use again. I promise you. My time with drugs is over. You're the only one I care about." He kissed her temple, and she smiled.

"Do you like Lynne and William?"

"Considering William is a lawyer I actually thought he was rather cool. I know, strange."

"He wasn't like any of the other lawyers she'd been with. There were some who'd criticize her on her fashion sense."

He shook his head. "Some people are crazy."

"I know." She chuckled. "Is this real right now?"

"We're real, baby."

"I love you."

"I love you, too." He kissed her again.

Turning in his arms she moved up his body, wrapping her arms around him. "Will I have to meet some of your old girlfriends?" she asked.

"Maybe. None of them are going to matter. You're going to see, and so are they, that you're the only one I care about."

He cupped her ass, and she wrapped her legs around his. Dick sat up, sinking his fingers into her hair, and gripping the back of her head. She moaned as he pulled on some of the strands. The small jolt of pain sent another shockwave of pleasure rushing through her entire body. She whimpered at the pleasure that consumed her, and she sank her fingers into his hair, gripping the short length.

Dick didn't push her away, he held her closer.

"I need you."

"I don't have a condom," he said.

"I don't care. I trust and love you. Please."

"I'm clean. I swear to you, baby, I'm clean."

"I'm clean as well."

She needed him more than she needed anything else.

They released each other, and she tore at her clothing. Dick did the same until they were both naked.

He took charge, yanking her toward him, banding his arms around her as he devoured her mouth. She was at his mercy, and she loved every second of it. No one was around to witness their fucking.

Dick pushed her to the ground, opening her thighs, and teasing her pussy with his tongue. He licked from her cunt up to her clit, circling the bud. She opened for him, relishing every touch of his tongue.

When he bit down hard on her clit, she cried out in pleasure. The pain was insignificant compared to the pleasure he was creating. He slid two fingers within her pussy, stretching her.

Suddenly, he changed, turning her so that she was on her knees before him. Glancing behind her, she saw his gaze was riveted to her ass. She wasn't going to complain, especially when his hands stroked over her ass.

"So fucking perfect. I'm going to fuck this pretty ass." He slapped one rounded cheek, going to the next, and spanking it once again. She whimpered from the pain but didn't move. Martha loved it when he spanked her. The pain always helped to turn her on.

He slid his hand between her legs, teasing her pussy with one finger. He slipped two fingers inside her pussy, and brought them back to her ass, pressing lightly. She moaned. At the same time as he pressed a finger to her ass, he started to ease his cock inside her pussy.

When the tip of him was inside her, he paused, making her wait. She wriggled trying to get him to go deeper, but he refused. He wouldn't let her move. Even with his finger teasing his ass, his other arm kept her close so that she didn't move.

The anticipation became too much, and she didn't think she could handle another second of waiting for his cock to take her.

She screamed out as Dick pounded his long, hard cock deep inside her. Sinking her fingers into the grass, she became the vessel for Dick's cock. His finger moved from her ass to be replaced with his thumb. He pressed inside, and even though it pinched, there was no overbearing pain. She took his thumb, and he fucked her pussy like a beast. He didn't stop.

"I need to make you forget everyone else. I need you only to remember my dick."

"I do. You're the only one I remember. Please, Dick, I love and need you. Fuck me. Fuck me. Fuck me."

He did, slamming into her over and over again, making her take every single inch of his cock until she couldn't think past the pain and combined pleasure of what he was doing. Dick pumped his dick into her pussy and fucked her ass with his thumb.

Reaching between her thighs, she stroked her clit, bringing herself to the peak of orgasm.

"You better not come until I tell you. I don't want to hear or feel you come yet."

She whimpered, begging him to let her find her release. He kept her poised at the edge never allowing her to go over.

Martha shook from the need that was consuming her.

Dick teased her without mercy.

"That's it, baby. Come for me. Let me feel how fucking tight and wet you can get. I want your pussy to squeeze me."

Stroking her clit twice, Martha came.

The strength of her release surprised her, taking her to a new edge of pleasure. It was like she lived to serve Dick.

****

On Monday morning after giving Lynne and William strict instructions on how to care for her garden, Dick finally took Martha to Piston County. The drive was a long and hard one as Martha kept getting nervous.

"What if they don't like me?" she asked.

"They're going to love you."

"How do you know that? You don't know that."

"I love you so they're going to love you."

He'd pull over and talk to her, calming her down. "Is this the first time you've got to go and meet some guy's family?"

"Yes."

Dick couldn't help but chuckle. "You're scared to meet the parents. I don't have any."

"They're your family though. They know what is good or bad for you, even if they're not related by blood."

Leaning across the car, Dick caught her face in his hands, and forced her to stare at him. "This is why I love you. You care, and the other women in my life didn't. They're going to love you. I'm scared as hell that they're all going to scare you off."

She let out a breath, which he found to be the most adorable thing of all.

"Okay, let's go."

For the next couple of hours he distracted her. First, he distracted her with talking about the garden. Next, he moved onto the house she'd love to have. He'd learned during his stay with her that the house was exactly in the way her parents wanted it. Dick planned for them both to move to Piston County, giving her a chance to make her dream home.

After that, he started talking about what he was going to do to her when he did finally get her home.

Fortunately, he pulled into the Chaos Bleeds parking lot during the completion of his fantasy, leaving her hot and bothered, and him horny as fuck.

Dick laughed when he saw the "Welcome Home" sign. He spotted Spider, Sinner, Death, Pussy, Ripper, Mia, Brianna, Judi all waiting at the door for him. They were waving and whooping for him.

"This is it," she said.

"They're going to love you."

"I'm warning you. I'm not very good with confrontation."

"Don't worry. The old ladies there will have your back." Dick climbed out of the car, and moved to her side. The crowd seemed to be in shock at his gentlemanly behavior as they all went silent. He took Martha's hand, locking their fingers together. "I won't let you go."

Devil and Lexie pulled into the parking lot. He stood waiting for his prez, and squeezed Martha's hand. She was shaking a little bit from the nerves.

"It's good to have you back," Devil said, pulling him in for a hug, and slapping his back.

"Hey, I'm Lexie."

"Martha."

The two women hugged tight. "I have to say we're all in a bit of a shock."

"I can imagine," Martha said. "He's told me what an asshole he can be. I warn you, he's not always an ass." Martha gave a wink, and the two women went into a fit of giggles.

"You look happy," Devil said.

"I am happy."

"Good."

When he reached out for Martha's hand, she placed hers within his, and together they walked toward the cluster of people, his brothers.

He started introducing all of them.

"This is Ripper, and his old lady, Judi. The little guy in her arms is Paul."

They were all amazed at Martha. He saw the shock they all had in their eyes.

Yeah, fuckers, I've got me a keeper.

"That's Curse and Mia. Pussy and Sasha." He whispered into her ear that Sasha was blind. "Death and Brianna, that fucker there is Snake, and Jessica."

"Dick, it's good to have you back," Vincent said.

"That's Vincent, and his old lady is Phoebe, but I don't see her."

"She's at home with the kids. They're ill so she couldn't make it," Vincent said.

He made sure that she saw the couples in the club before introducing her to the club whores, and the guys who weren't attached.

It didn't take long for Lydia to split apart from the group. He noticed she'd been sitting with Dime and Butler. Both men didn't look happy with Lydia.

"Hey, baby, I've been waiting for you to get back."

When she made to wrap her arms around him, he tugged Martha in front of him. She froze in his arms, and Lydia just glared. "You've got to be fucking kidding me," she said. "You're going to get rid of me for a fat fucking bitch. She's homely."

Dick tensed.

"Fuck off, Lydia," Jessica said. "He doesn't want you. The club doesn't want you here. They've put up with you because of him. It's time you left."

Lydia's mouth opened wide. "I can't believe you're actually doing this."

"Believe it, baby. I've not wanted you in a long time. You wouldn't listen to me, and now I'm having to deal with you the only way I know how."

"By being a dick," Lydia said.

"Yes, by being a dick."

"Are you prepared to fight me for him?" Lydia asked.

All eyes turned on Martha. Dick tensed. She'd been fighting her whole life against her sister, and failed.

"I'm not going to fight you," Martha said.

"You're going to trade me in for a bitch who won't even fight for you."

"No, I'll fight for Dick. The truth is, you've already lost. He's mine, and you're making yourself look stupid by thinking he'd take you otherwise. Dick doesn't want you. He gave you a chance to make friends with Jessica, not to annoy him. You've started annoying him, and you've got to move on."

Dick released a sigh. She was right. He belonged to Martha, just like Martha belonged to him. There was no way in hell he was giving up his woman.

"What about Master? You can't just leave me out there."

"I didn't say you had to leave," Dick said,

knowing that Master was a real threat. The bastard would come out of the woodwork eventually. Men like that always did. "I'm taken. This is my woman, and you need to back off."

Lydia nodded, taking a step back.

When he looked at all of his brothers, he saw they agreed, and also confirmed to him without asking that Master still hadn't been located. This also confirmed that Master had a shitload of money at his disposal, and none of them were ever going to get close enough to him until he was ready to come out and play.

"You can stay at the clubhouse, Lydia, I'm not going to send you out when we don't know what Master is doing," Devil said, grabbing Lydia's arm. "You cause any problems for us, and I let you go."

"I won't cause any problems," she said. "What do I do?"

"You will work at the clubhouse. Whatever anyone wants you to do, do it. I hear shit from you, I'll handle you myself. Do I make myself clear?"

Devil was threatening, and Martha felt bad for Lydia, but the other woman simply nodded, and was released.

When Lydia was gone, all the attention turned back to Dick.

Martha was taken away from him as the brothers tugged him in close.

"What the fuck was that gentlemanly act?" Sinner asked. "I thought you were the dick in the group. Not opening doors for bitches."

"She's not a bitch. She's mine." He slugged Sinner in the stomach. Glancing out of the window, he saw the women had taken Martha to the small little play area that they'd built for the kids.

"She looks like a good one, a keeper," Devil said.

"She is." He turned back to look at his Prez. "She keeps me sane."

"It's what we've got to do, find a woman who makes us want to be sane." Devil looked into the yard, clearly staring at Lexie. "I was half a fucking man when I met Lex. She made me whole. She gives me something to fight for, and to fight harder than ever before."

Dick nodded, finally understanding what Devil was saying. All of these years he'd watched each of his brothers fall for a woman, and all the time, he'd not understood what it actually meant to be in love, really in love.

"Come on," Devil said.

Turning to the rest of the brothers, he took their hugs, and acceptance of him back. "What about the house?" he asked, turning back to Devil.

"It's yours." Devil tossed the keys into the air, and he caught them.

"Thank you."

"You've got to show her your place yet, and then convince her to stay. "You've got a hell of a fight on your hands."

Taking a seat at the bar, he opened a can of soda, and took a drink. From the moment he'd seen Martha again, the urge to do drugs had disappeared. He didn't want to go down that slippery slope. He was a man in charge of his own destiny. No matter what he'd done in the past, Martha accepted him for the present, and the future he was going to give.

"Hey, man," Spider said.

"Hey, yourself. What's going on with you?"

"Hasn't he told you?" Death asked.

"Told me what?" Dick looked at his brothers, and they were smiling.

"I've been helping Paris."

"The woman that works at the strip club?"

"Yeah. It turns out her parents were two of the civilians that were hurt in the shootout at Fort Wills. She's taking care of her sister who was born with brain damage. They were twins."

"Wow, shit, I've missed a lot."

"Yeah." Spider looked deep in thought.

It was a look that Dick wouldn't have associated with Spider. "What's up?"

"Nothing. She's been fighting for the last couple of years, you know? She got custody of her sister, and is taking care of her. We've provided the protection she needs. She doesn't have to work at the club anymore. I'm taking care of her expenses and shit."

"Spider, that's a commitment, buddy."

"I know. I can't just walk away."

"Are you telling me you've got feelings for her?"

"I've got something," Spider said. "I don't know what it is, and it's not just about getting laid. Sure, she's a pretty and all, fucking hard as rock for her when she danced. It's different now. She's not putting on a show."

"You've seen the woman inside, not the woman that is portrayed on the stage?" Dick asked.

"Yeah. Once you've seen that, there's no going back."

"How come she's not here now?"

Spider shrugged. "She doesn't trust us."

"That's fucking harsh, considering you're helping her."

"She's all alone with a sister to protect. She doesn't know me other than I'm the guy who watched her dance." Spider took a sip of his soda. "I'm going to go and see her. It's great to have you back, man."

"It's great to be back even if I am a little in the dark."

He didn't like being in the dark, but this wasn't part of Spider's choice. The brother had a lot of weight on his shoulders. It was easier when you didn't care. The drugs helped to numb that part of him that cared. For the longest time, he didn't give a shit about anyone, or anything. Like Martha said when talking about Becky and her parents, there comes a time when everything catches up with you. Spider, and even himself, had found that time.

****

Spider knocked on the door waiting to be let in. Paris opened the door, and even though she gave him a small smile, there was still that hesitancy inside her.

"Hey," she said.

"Hey. Sorry I didn't swing by earlier. One of the brothers is back, and he brought his woman with him for us to meet," Spider said.

He wasn't used to having to make excuses, even though it wasn't an excuse. This was the truth.

"I'm not your keeper, Spider."

"I wanted to come and see you and Celia to find out how you're doing."

Paris stared at him for several seconds. "I'm not going to sleep with you. If this offer of support, and help, is to sleep with me, then you're very much mistaken."

"It's not," Spider said.

"Oh."

"Don't get me wrong, I want to sleep with you, but this isn't about that, I promise." Spider rubbed the back of his head, looking around the neighborhood. "Are you going to let me in?"

"Yes, sorry."

She opened the door a little wider, and the sound of Celia from the kitchen moaning had Paris turning away from him.

This was his chance to turn and walk away. Spider stared at the door, and listened to Paris comforting her sister, her twin. He took a deep breath, and went to leave, but he couldn't move. Spider couldn't go back. There was no life without Paris, and in that moment, he realized he had to stay. He needed to have Paris in his life.

Chapter Ten

"I can't believe you're with Dick. He's like a big, giant asshole," Jessica said.

Martha laughed. All of the women were talking about Dick, but she saw the affection they all had for him. He had his place in Chaos Bleeds, just like every other brother.

"Do you love him?" Lexie asked.

"Yes, I love him. I know it's crazy, and insane, and totally out of the realm of my understanding." Martha took the drink that Mia offered her.

"You've known each other like a week," Jessica said.

"No, not a week. A couple of years ago when he went to rehab that's when I first got to know him."

"And you liked him?" This came from Judi.

"He was nice. My sister was in rehab, and she wasn't handling it well through withdrawal. Anyway, he was nice, and he helped me in ways that Becky, my sister, didn't."

"Where is your sister now?" Brianna asked.

"She didn't make it. A couple of months after getting out of rehab, she OD'ed. I watched, and I was trapped in place." She shrugged, taking a sip of her drink. "There wasn't anything I could have done." Martha explained to them what happened.

"Damn, honey, that is harsh."

"It's okay. Seeing Dick, and being with him, he makes my world spin." Martha smiled at each woman in turn.

"You're not going to pull him away, are you?" Lexie asked. "I know he's a dick, and he annoys me, and I want to shout at him, but he's still family. I couldn't be without him."

"I don't know what's going to happen. I've got a home, and I don't know where we go from here," Martha said.

"How about we take a little trip?" Dick said, interrupting their conversation.

She looked toward him to see him dangling a set of keys.

"What do you have in mind?" she asked.

"I want to take you for a little ride."

Handing Lexie her cup, Martha gave each woman a hug. "It was a pleasure to meet you all."

"And you." They all spoke together.

She took Dick's hand that he offered her, and followed him back toward the car. "We only just got here," she said.

"I know. There's something I want to show you, and I don't want to wait another moment." He opened the passenger door for her, and she climbed inside waiting for him.

Dick pulled out of the parking lot minutes later, and they were traveling down a long dirt road.

"Do you miss this?" she asked.

"This is my home."

He missed it, and Martha wondered how they were going to live together. Dick had a life here, and she had a home miles away. It wasn't much of a life, and she didn't want to be part of the world that Becky had created for her. What Charles did to her a few nights ago was a regular occurrence in her life.

They passed through a town which suddenly opened up. She saw some rather large, beautiful houses.

"This is where Lexie and Devil live. Vincent and Phoebe also live close by." He pulled up outside a house that looked pretty vacant. Work needed doing in the back yard, and before she could stop herself, Martha was already redesigning the yard. She'd picked out three different sets of roses, and several stones that she'd keep as features.

"What's going on?" she asked.

They were outside, heading toward the front door. Martha's heart was racing as she tried to take it all in. Everything was happening so fast, and the world was once again spinning.

This was what Dick did.

He made her feel alive.

Taking her hand, he opened the front door.

"Go on inside."

"Do you own this?" she asked.

"Tell me what you think."

"I'm a little confused right now. I don't know what to think or what to make of what is happening." She tucked some hair behind her ear as they made their way around the house. It was empty, and there was a lot of work that needed to be done.

He took her hand, leading her toward the back yard. "We can have a life together here."

"Dick—"

"Listen to me."

She watched as he unlocked the door, and pulled her out toward the garden. The beauty before her took her breath away. To a lot of people the yard looked like an overgrown mess. Martha saw a blank canvas that she could make all of her own. No one would have made the foundations within this garden. This could be all of hers, with no one else having their designs.

"I found your sketchbook, and I saw that you've got a vision of your own dream house with a dream garden for everything. I want to make your dream come true."

"Dick, what are you saying?" she asked.

"I'm asking you, in a strange, weird way, to marry me."

She gasped, turning toward him. "You're asking me to marry you?"

"Yes. I want you to marry me. I want to spend the rest of my life with you. There's nothing else that I want more than to grow old with you, to fall in love with you, and just be with you."

"I couldn't pull you away from your club. They're great people."

She'd only seen them for a few minutes, but Martha saw the truth of the club. Chaos Bleeds were united together, how a family was supposed to be.

"I want you to be part of that, be part of the club with me."

Tears filled her eyes, and Martha just wrapped her arms around his neck, holding him close.

"I love you."

"I love you, too, baby. I love you so much." He held her tightly to him. "Does this mean you're going to marry me?"

"Yes, it's a big, fat yes. Of course I'm going to marry you. I love you, and there's no one else I'd rather be with than you." She gripped the back of his neck, slamming her lips down on his. Dick sank his fingers into her hair, and she melted against him, needing his heat, and warmth surrounding her.

"I've got one question for you," she said.

"What is it?"

"Does this house belong to you?"

He chuckled. "Yes, I called ahead. This house is mine, and no one is taking it away from us."

"Then I'll take it, and I'll take you."

****

"Did you see the way they looked at each other?"

Jessica asked.

"They're in love. I bet they're married before the end of the year," Judi said.

Lexie smiled, looking around at all of the women. This was the family she loved, and it looked like they were about to have another woman added to the mix. She left the girls alone to talk about Martha. Lexie found Devil in their room overlooking the grounds. They would have to go and get Simon soon.

"Are you okay?"

"Yeah."

"What is it?" she asked, walking up behind him, rubbing his back.

"Everything is changing. Dick's in love. Who thought that man was going to find love?"

"He's surprised us all."

Devil tugged her in front of her. Something didn't sit right with her when Devil got like this. He was staring out of the window, looking down on the women and some of the men who walked out to join them.

"What's going on, Devil?"

"Something is about to happen, Lex. I don't know what, and I don't know when, but it's going to be soon."

Fear gripped her. Devil had these feelings, and he'd always been right before.

"I don't know what to say to you right now," she said. Tears filled her eyes.

"I'm not asking you to say anything." He turned her toward him, cupping her face. "I love you with all my heart."

"Devil?"

"He's going to come for us, Lex."

"Who?"

"Master. He's going to come for us, and I've already talked to Tiny. You're going to live with him when it happens."

"Okay, this is too much. You're getting afraid."

Devil released her, and walked toward an envelope that she'd not seen, resting on their bed. He handed it to her.

Frowning, she took the envelope from him, opening it up.

Lexie froze.

A message had been written on a single white sheet of paper.

I'm coming for you.

M x

The message wasn't what scared her. Beneath the message were six pictures, all of them of the women that had recently married. Lexie stood with her kids, holding Simon's hand. Judi was holding her baby, but what scared Lexie most was this was taken outside of Judi's home, near the window. There was one of Mia walking down the street. Sasha was with her dog and walking stick. Brianna was in her bedroom in her photograph, and then Jessica was coming outside of the hospital for hers.

"He's coming for us. He's coming for our women, Lex."

"We can fight him."

"I can't fight a ghost. This is what that man is, a ghost. I'm taking the men to church, and when I do, we're going to act."

Rushing into Devil's arms, Lexie held onto the man she'd come to love. She trusted him with her life, and if he said bad things were about to happen, she listened.

Master was coming, and it was only a matter of time before he came for them.

****

Dick was anxious to get back to Martha. He'd left

her in his room while he attended church. Everyone was sitting around the table, and Devil was just silent. Dick had been home for the entire day, and he'd been shocked when church had been announced.

"What's going on?" Curse asked.

"Martha's agreed to marry me," Dick said, speaking up. He couldn't contain it any longer. He wanted the whole world to know that Martha was going to be his.

All of the brothers offered him congratulations, which he took. He was so damn happy that he could just burst. Dick couldn't recall a time he'd ever been happier than he was now.

"We can't have any celebrations yet," Devil said.

"Why not?" Dick asked, tensing up.

Even if they didn't like Martha, it wasn't up to them.

"This is why."

Devil dropped a piece of paper with a message, along with several photographs. The room went silent as the men took in the evidence.

"Master?" Dick asked.

"Yes."

"He's watching us," Death said, gripping the picture of Brianna in his fist.

"This isn't watching. This is fucking taunting." Snake grabbed Jessica's picture and tore it in two. "I'm not going to fucking take this. The bastard can go and fucking rot."

"This threat is real," Devil said.

They all went silent when Devil said that.

"Real? They're a bunch of pictures," Sinner said.

"You've not got a woman being threatened here. This Master guy is a real threat, and we don't know anything about him. He's real, and he's coming for us.

We pissed him off by shutting his supply of girls down. We can't risk ignoring this shit."

Devil ran a hand down his face, showing all of the brothers how serious this threat was.

"I've been talking with Tiny. Whizz has alerted him to the danger that surrounds us with this. I want the women to go to Fort Wills until we know what is happening."

The silence was deafening.

Dick slapped his hands down on the table. "Done. Whatever we need to do to protect the women, and our kids, we do it. The Skulls, we've had our differences with them, but we've got to overcome that shit to find the right path."

Devil nodded at him.

"We don't know anything about him," Death said. "He's winning left and right."

"That's very true, but he's given us something that he may not realize he's given us," Devil said.

"What?" Snake asked.

Devil picked up the photograph of Sasha and pointed at the time and date on the bottom of the photograph. "He's given us a location, a time, and a date. Whizz can access these records, and we can find out who is working for him. It's not a lot, but it's a start."

They all sat and talked for a long time, and Dick was shocked when Devil finally announced that the wedding between him and Martha would take place.

"It can't be a lavish affair, Dick, but if you're prepared to wait then I can get Tiny to make sure there's a ceremony in Fort Wills."

"Okay," Dick said.

Minutes later church was dismissed, and Dick walked upstairs to Martha. The moment she saw him, she opened her arms. He locked the world behind him, wrapping his arms around his woman, and holding her close.

"What's the matter?" she asked.

"Some things are about to change."

"Should I be scared?"

"No. I'm going to protect you."

Instead of keeping everything from her, Dick shared his fear, and everything that was happening. When he was finished, he stared into her eyes. "I will understand if you want to run back home. This life, it can be scary."

She cupped his cheek and ran her thumb across his lip.

"I'm not here for the fun of it, Dick. I'm here because you're the love of my life. There's a threat to the club, and to my man, I guess I'm going to have to fight beside him."

"You're not going to leave?"

"I'm not going to leave. I'm with you through thick and thin. We may not have said our vows, but I mean them now. To me, Dick, we're a married couple."

"You're not scared?"

"I'm a little scared. Life is a little scary, but I'm not going to run away. I'm going to stay by your side, through the good and the bad. I love you."

She pressed her lips to his, and Dick knew he'd found the woman for him.

Epilogue

Spider made his way out of the clubhouse. He didn't like the bad omen that Devil was getting. His Prez had yet to be wrong about something like that. It had to be true, as otherwise Devil wouldn't have gotten in touch with Tiny.

The Skulls and Chaos Bleeds hadn't been the best of friends for some time now. Devil still visited Fort Wills, but he did that for Lexie. The tension was always there.

Climbing onto his bike, Spider knew where he wanted to go. He'd left Paris and Celia that afternoon to come back for church. Now that church was done, he was going back to see them. He couldn't make a move with Paris now.

The threat of Master saw to that.

Riding toward her house, he knew he was going to request that Paris and Celia be moved with the women. He didn't know if anyone was watching him visit the two, and he wouldn't put either of them in danger.

Parking his bike up outside of her house, he made his way toward the front door. Spider raised his hand and froze. There, nailed to the door, was an envelope. His heart raced, and he grabbed his cell phone, dialing the club.

He was shocked when Devil answered.

"Hello," he said.

"You need to come to Paris's house." He gave the address and reached out for the envelope. "He's been here, Devil."

Opening up the envelope he saw the message first.

Come and find me, if you can.
M x

Underneath was a picture of Celia and Paris. Both women were curled up together on the sofa fast asleep.

Entering the house, Spider looked around the room. There had been a struggle, and he spotted blood on the carpet along with a torn piece of Paris's shirt.

Kneeling beside the blood, he wished he had some kind of fucking super-sense. He was panicking that they'd taken his woman.

The sound of a gunshot rang in the air, and pain laced through Spider's shoulder. Placing his hand to his shoulder, he turned, and as he did, another bullet shot him in the leg, making him fall to the floor.

"Now, I've got your attention," a man said, coming toward him.

Spider didn't recognize him, but he knew that he had to be working for Master in some way. He didn't recognize the man as the Master that the women spoke of. He didn't get it. "Who the fuck are you?" he asked.

"Ah, you know I'm not Master, then?"

The man before him was a good-looking man who didn't need to buy women against their will. Spider didn't know if Master was good looking or not. "A guy with a lot of money as his disposal wouldn't come here in person."

"You're right. I work for Master, and you can call me 'Sir'. I have a message from Master."

"What?" Spider asked.

"Chaos Bleeds wants to hunt for me, find me, and ruin me, that's fine. I like playing games, and this is going to be my first game, hide and seek. You live past this night, and I will have Celia delivered to you without harm." Sir smiled. "I was always good at delivering messages word for word."

"Paris," Spider said, pressing a hand to his shoulder. His leg was going to be a problem. If the bastard got the femoral artery, he was fucked.

"Like I said, live past this night, you get Celia, and the rules to part two. Until then, try to stay alive."

Another shot rang out, and Spider screamed. He'd been shot in the leg again, and he had to fight. Spider had to hold on.

Master had his woman, and he needed to get her back. There was another player as well, Sir. What was it with all the fucking Dom names?

Screaming at the top of his lungs, Spider tried to stay alive, but sleep was calling him.

Everything was going dark.

Stay alive.

The End

www.samcrescent.com

BROKEN HEARTS

EVERNIGHT PUBLISHING ®

www.evernightpublishing.com